NEVER'S JUST THE ECHO
OF FOREVER

BARRY CALLAGHAN

NEVER'S
just the
ECHO
of
FOREVER

INTRODUCTION BY
LEON ROOKE

BOOK ONE OF THE
SWEETWATER CALHOUN SERIES

EXILE
editions

singular fiction, poetry, nonfiction, translation, drama, and graphic books

Library and Archives Canada Cataloguing in Publication

Title: Never's just the echo of forever / Barry Callaghan ; introduction by
    Leon Rooke.
Other titles: Never is just the echo of forever
Names: Callaghan, Barry, 1937- author. | Rooke, Leon, writer of introduction.
Description: Series statement: Sweetwater Calhoun series ; book one
Identifiers: Canadiana (print) 20230485286 | Canadiana (ebook) 20230485332 |
    ISBN 9781550969610 (softcover) | ISBN 9781550969634 (Kindle) |
    ISBN 9781550969641 (PDF) | ISBN 9781550969627 (EPUB)
Classification: LCC PS8555.A49 N48 2023 | DDC C813/.54—dc23

This is a work of fiction; therefore, the novel's story and characters are fictitious.
    Any public agencies, institutions, or historical figures mentioned in the story serve
    as a backdrop to the characters and their actions, which are wholly imaginary.

The Sweetwater Calhoun Series, and all Exile Editions books, are published
    independantly of financial assistance from the Canada Council for the Arts's
    or the Ontario Arts Council's Book Publishing: Block Grant programs.

Canadian sales representation:
The Canadian Manda Group, 664 Annette Street, Toronto ON M6S 2C8
www.mandagroup.com 416 516 0911

North American and international distribution, and U.S. sales:
Independent Publishers Group, 814 North Franklin Street,
Chicago IL 60610 www.ipgbook.com toll free: 1 800 888 4741

for beloved Claire
who is my past ever present,
and my beloved boys,
Kellen and Kaedán,
who are my future

INTRODUCTION
by
LEON ROOKE

Toward the end of this immensely powerful novella, a sleazy reporter snaps a photo that will later appear with a story whose headline is "THE CROSSING GUARD NOBODY KNOWS." The unwilling subject, the novella's hero, has recently lost his job as a crossing guard for schoolchildren but can't stop doing what he's meant to do, so now he helps assorted others, mostly old folks, to get safely to the other side: "Stopping traffic, helping people all day just for the sake of helping them, it's a terrific human interest story. It'll cheer our readers up."

The chilling banality of that term aside, a terrific human interest story is exactly what *Never's Just the Echo of Forever* is. For all the pain and terror encountered here, it should also cheer the reader up to experience this gorgeously wrought, profoundly tender piece of work. This may well be Barry Callaghan's best story, and certainly it is one of the most perfectly accomplished and haunting Canadian fictions that I know. The central character, this crossing guard nobody knows, this man always on the brink of never, is known in the end by Callaghan so deeply, with such vast compassion, that by rights he ought to go on forever.

Albie Starbach is 34, a caretaker for a Toronto rooming house and caregiver for his crippled mother as well as a crossing guard: thus, thrice over, marked as one who gives. For much of the story the word "grief" haunts Albie; later a second word, "give," becomes its companion. Together they go to the heart of Albie's achievement as a human being, which truth persists despite the violence that overtakes him. For all that he has lost or never had, for all the torment and craziness he seeks to hold at bay, he is a man of great sweetness, true generosity.

Albie is haunted also by a constellation of obsessive images and by a pair of old "desperados," invisible to others, sad-eyed gunslingers out of the cowboy myth that he lives amid the steel and glass canyons of Toronto streets. This is very much a poet's novella; Callaghan is, of course, a brilliant poet as well as a powerful storyteller – part of the strong Canadian contingent of genre-crossers that includes Margaret Atwood and Michael Ondaatje. Like them, he uses image patterns of great complexity and tensile strength to build his fiction and to make it sing.

Interestingly, there is a strong similarity at the level of image and in the handling of insanity and violence between Callaghan's novella and Ondaatje's *Coming Through Slaughter*, especially at the stunning close of each. The two heroes are wildly different men, but each comes through slaughter (inner torment, his own violence, and the ugliest of external realities) to a place where he can no longer be touched by it; each crosses over safely to a place that only those who enter the character fully with the author will know is one of beauty.

The world of this novella is dangerous, an explosive desert storm both in the microcosm of Albie's mind and in the geopolitical surround reflected by his mother's viewing of war in the Middle East. Spectral gunslingers hang from the trees, a train will come at High Noon to a town with only one defender, the gift of sexuality goes dark, and in a furnace room the voices of the doomed are channelled through air ducts to the dangerous, gentle man who waits at the centre of it all. But Callaghan also maintains for Albie and for the reader, on the other side and sometimes here, an alternative world of natural beauty, tenderness, and spiritual peace. And this is conveyed not only through the imagery of a yearning imagination but by the reality of the characters.

Best of all is the lovely relationship of mother and son, through which the balm of humour also comes into play. Astonishing Emma Rose, her palm bleeding stigmata-like years after being nailed by a knife-thrower lover's errant blade, lifting dumb-bells so that she "looked like a fugitive from the law practicing to surrender at gunpoint," walking on her hands in the basement apartment, her poor crippled legs dancing in the air, or refreshed by the breeze during outings with her good son on a Toronto ferry boat, is a magnificent creation. There is also wonderful Sebastien, the boy who loves and wants to be like Albie, who puts lipstick on so that the face of his lost mother in the mirror can assure him that she loves him. And there is Yuri, substitute father and lover of Emma Rose when Albie was 19, who put cowboy boots on his feet and taught him what he learned himself in a Nazi concentration camp – the need to concentrate.

The rich theme of the lost father is central here. Albie has never known his father, but he is a thorough mensch in spite of that: eminently trustworthy employee and good family man to his mother, the lonely dwellers in the rooming house, and the children on the street. The lost father, Yuri, and the old desperados merge, and are linked to another lost father who is "WANTED DEAD OR ALIVE: GOD." Albie wonders if God (who "saw all there was to see with the freshness of vision in which nothing was hid") wasn't in him, together with "God's words, because out of nowhere, the dark waters at the back of his mind would part and he'd see with utter clarity… a crease in the face of a weathered old man, or an unlaced shoe, and wings, white wings, and flying fish." But the angels, he would know in his heart –

though "they had lived and flown and fought with each other in the sky" – were gone now, "scissored out" of a picture that has been left full of holes.

In the end, Albie eats the words of God in a beautifully ambiguous act – and the anger inside him shrivels, so that "there was not an angry bone left in his body" and the words from Apocalypse that Callaghan uses as the epigraph for this beautiful work are fulfilled: "And I went unto the angel, and said unto him, Give me the little book. And he said unto me, Take it, and eat it up; and it shall make thy belly bitter, but it shall be in thy mouth as sweet as honey." So it is with the transformative power of this little book. Take it, then, and read.

And I went unto the angel, and said unto him, Give me the little book. And he said unto me, Take it, and eat it up; and it shall make thy belly bitter, but it shall be in thy mouth sweet as honey.

And I took the little book out of the angel's hand, and ate it up; and it was in my mouth sweet as honey: and as soon as I had eaten it, my belly was bitter.

—APOCALYPSE 10: 9-10

As Albie Starbach stood at the foot of the stairs to the stone house, he heard a lone sweet fiddle high in the bare trees. He had dark red hair, hazel eyes, and strong bony hands, and as he stared at the melting snow and the slush in the flagstone gutters, he pulled on his heavy, saddle-stitched sheepskin gloves. He liked to keep his hands warm. He picked up a round paddle that had STOP painted on it in fluorescent red, and he wore a red vest that was fluorescent, too, saying softly to himself *sashay, sashay,* liking the sound of the word but he wasn't sure whether a man should ever want to sashay, so he strode down the walk, pretending to ignore a grizzled old desperado who was standing in the snow under the apple tree, an old desperado who craned his neck and whispered, "Albie, Albie, there are people dying who've never died before." Albie shrugged, not breaking his stride though he knew the slush would soak a salt ring into his black cowboy boots, and the salt would then rot the leather, but there was nothing he could do because he knew salt was tougher than leather. "Cowboys don't wear no damn hip waders," he had told his mother, but she'd scowled and said, "You ain't no cowboy, you're a caretaker. You got cowboys beating on your poor addled brain." He tucked a chaw of Old Chum tobacco in his cheek and said, "Salt is even tougher than love." A red snow shovel stood against the trunk of the apple tree. The blade was rusted. There were twisted black apples on the tree. The old desperado began to sing, "*A-may…zing grace, how sweet the sound…*" as Albie looked at the shovel and then back to the big house, the old cut lime-stone walls stained by the weeping iron in the stone and the tiny crab-like tracks of the ivy he'd ripped from the walls, enraged at starlings who'd built hidden nests in the leaves. He laughed. "Some caretaker. If I was the owner, I'd goddamn well fire myself."

～ 2 ～

He had nervous hands and quick eyes. He narrowed his eyes whenever he walked alone into a bar in the early hours of the morning, trying to slit his eyes like a snake. He was sure that all the old gunslingers had looked down at the dead lying in the dust like that. Snake eyes. And cops, too. Snakes were smart and so were cops. Nobody played cops or snakes for fools. As a boy, he'd had a snake tattooed on his left forearm and he had thought about being a cop, a cop packing a snub-nose .38 in a shoulder-holster close to his heart because he wanted to see and feel things with the hard-nosed grit of a cop, and he had watched all the gunslinger and gumshoe shows on television, all the reruns of *Law and Order*, and *Kojak,* and *The Rifleman,* and Harry Callahan and his Magnum .44, looking to see who had the most grit, who could hand out the most grief, but then one afternoon he'd been arrested for shoplifting. It was the day before his 20th birthday. He had got up in the morning and with his finger he'd drawn 19 in the film of dust on his bedroom window, intending to wash the window clean the next day, and intending to start a whole new life as his own man in his 20s, and then he'd gone out to buy himself a birthday present. He had picked up a white Stetson hat in a western clothing store, but he'd also seen a pair of turquoise cufflinks set in silver in a glass showcase and, not wanting to soil the hat on the top of the showcase, he'd stuck the hat on his head and studied the veins in the turquoise and then he'd bought the cufflinks and walked out of the store. He'd started to sing:

> The red-headed stranger had eyes like thunder,
> and his lips they were sad and tight,
> his little lost love lay on the hillside
> and his heart was heavy as night:
> Don't cross him, don't boss him,
> he's wild in his sorrow...

They'd stopped him on the sidewalk, the fat waddly owner of the store and a cop. He'd narrowed his eyes. If he'd been a snake, he would have bitten them in the throat. He couldn't understand the shopkeeper's anger. He couldn't understand the cop's sneering contempt. Anger seemed to be loose in the air. Like everybody had a secret beef, like they wanted to get even. So usually he was on the watch, on the lookout all the time for whoever was going to hurt him for no good reason. Hurt was what people wanted to do. He tried to tell the cop as calmly as he could, "I forgot. The hat was on top of my head." An old desperado sidled out of the boarded-up Le Coq d'Or saloon and laughed. He laughed loudly, and he had brown broken teeth. Albie could see that he was a desperado who had come down through the dog years of dust and tumbleweed in the old ghost towns, a desperado who'd earned the right to sit with his arms folded in the sun and wait for the noon train, but even so, Albie told him to shut up. The burly cop slapped Albie and Albie said with bewildered astonishment, "I wasn't talking to you." The cop snarled, "What are you, some kinda slopehead? There ain't no one else but us here, you fucking smart ass." Albie saw the saloon's padlocked door and the sign,

CLOSED. The cop shouldered him into a corner, and so he said again, "I forgot, that's all. Hell, there's things even on top of your head you got to be able to forget." The cop snickered and said, "If your momma don't screw your head on to your neck, you'll forget it, too." The cop had a line of sweat pimples on his cheek. Albie believed pimples were the sign of a wanker's brain. He believed men got pimples from too much wanking and then stuffing their semen-shot socks and handkerchiefs down behind steaming radiators in the winter. He knew the reek of semen on his hands. He also knew the smell of women. He'd tasted the smell of women. It was like the damp earth where mushrooms cluster at the foot of hemlock trees and at the same time it somehow tasted of sweetened saltwater, like the raw fish he'd once eaten in a restaurant where he'd said, "This tastes just like you Elizabeth," smiling warmly at a waitress he often talked to, and he was sure – looking at the pimples on his cheek – that the wanker cop did not know about things like that, didn't know how to think in any way delicate about them, and he was so hurt by the cop's contempt that he kept his head down, staring at the desperado's boots, secretly satisfied because he knew that the cop would never be able to see the old unshaven gunslinger either, not the way that he could see him, the lines in his leathery sun-creased face, lines that came from sleeping lonely and travelling light for years with a weight of grief in his heart. Albie hunkered down into a weary, sullenly pained and sorrowful resignation, as if he'd known all along that the cops would disappoint him, and he thought it was a sign of his own growing up and grit and backbone that he'd so quickly come to accept such disappointment with a wry smile. "Disappointments like your Buckley's cough medicine," he'd told his crippled mother, "you swallow it to kill the tickle."

After the arrest he'd come home and washed the dirt and the number 19 from the window in his room, and he'd turned 20 quietly, but he'd also decided that 19 would be his unlucky number for the rest of his life. A month later when he was working as a bicycle courier, he got fired because he refused to make a delivery, refused to get off an elevator at the 19th floor. And then, that same week, he was convicted in night court by a bald-headed judge who didn't even bother to glance up at him. He was convicted of shoplifting. "If I'd wanted to be a criminal, I'd have been a criminal under my own hat," he'd said to the judge as the judge gathered his robes and read out in a low sonorous voice, "Since they tell me this man Starbach has no history, suspended sentence," and after that, Albie had always spoken resentfully of the cops and courts. "They don't know dick, they don't know nothing, which is why they're so dead-certain about what they don't know." He now refused to watch cop shows on television and he was glad when he heard that the old FBI head toadie, J. Edgar Hoover, liked to wear a dress and hold the hand of his second-banana-in-command, Clyde Tolson. "The fucking dick-licking fraud. They carry on like they're smarter than every other dickhead wanker," he said. If cops drove through his traffic crossing lane when there was a lot of traffic, he acted like he didn't see them and tucked his STOP sign under his arm and stared grimly ahead. If the street was empty, then he waved them through, furiously wigwagging his STOP sign like he was directing them to the scene of a crime. The puzzled looks on their faces, as though they thought he was harmlessly crazy, made him laugh. He knew he was not harmless and he believed he had every right to be crazy and laugh, just like he had the right to hear sweet fiddle music in the high branches if he wanted to. After all, it was his crossing lane, and he knew he was a good crossing guard, always on time, three times a day.

He had applied for the job after seeing it posted on the telephone pole in front of the stone house, but then he had been afraid that they would find out about the shoplifting conviction, that it would show up on a computer. Computers were how they knew about everything and everybody. He didn't care about the conviction itself and he could hardly remember the mustard-yellow courtroom or the bald judge. He remembered the hat. He was haunted by the hat, a white Stetson with an orange and black oriole's feather in the black, braided suede band. He saw the hat in his dreams. Sometimes he dreamt of trees full of hats, hats fluttering like birds, mourning doves. Though his favourite country singers all wore hats, and though he wore tailored western clothes with pearl-grey piping on the pockets when he went out at night to the local clubs or to the Zanzibar saloon on Saturday afternoons, he'd never worn a hat again, not even in the winter sleet or freezing rain. In fact, he liked the cold clarity of rainwater running out of his dark red hair and down his face. He could vision himself standing tall on a shelf of stone in the high country, standing against the long low clouded sky over the tundra. Staring into the wind. Narrowing his eyes against the grit on the wind, swollen with anger, an anger that sometimes pounded at the back of his head and gave him a headache. A jackhammer headache. He could bear headaches and the cold wind on his bare head and he didn't mind his wet feet soaking in his cowboy boots. But cold hands frightened him. When his big bony hands were cold, he lost all feeling in his fingers, and this, he thought, this numbness was as close to death as he could come without dying, not being able to feel the trembling of his own body in his fingertips.

One night, after he'd been with a woman in a dark hallway, a woman almost as old as his mother in her middle 50s, a woman he'd picked up in a bar and had fondled up against the wall, probing and pushing deep into her with two fingers until she'd said, "I'm happy. I'm happy. I don't want to fuck. Men weigh too much," he'd gone home and studied his fingertips under his bedside lamplight, prodding the pads of soft pale flesh that looked withered and drawn and bloodless after so long in the wet heat of the woman, and he'd been frustrated at not being able to see the inward swirl of lines he knew were there in his skin, so the next day he'd bought an ink pad at Woolworth's and had taken his own thumbprints on a sheet of blank white letter paper. "It's like seeing who you are," he'd told his mother, "your prints are pasted on the empty air." He'd thumb-tacked the paper to the wall at the foot of his bed, and sometimes he went to sleep staring at the two smudges in the dimmed light, his hazel eyes flecked with yellow. His mother had told him when he was a child that the yellow flecks were blind spots. There were things, she'd said, that he would never be able to see or understand. He had refused to believe her. One night when he'd found her alone and drunk and crying in her bed, he'd said, "I can see everything real clear, and look at you, you're a mess. You're drunk." She'd wiped her nose with the back of her hand and said, "You got a cruel eye, you're a cruel boy." He'd resented that, so he said, "No, I'm not. I love you because you're my mom. I only said I can see what I see, and you're sick drunk," and he'd broken into tears and gone back to his own bed where an hour later he suddenly sat up and that was the first time that he saw through the tumbleweed blowing across the end of the bed an old desperado gunslinger, his arms folded, his eyes full of wilted flowers.

⟞ 3 ⟝

Albie didn't sleep well. He never slept well, dreaming of swollen waters full of broken tree branches and drowning fish, and he shifted from shoulder to shoulder when he slept, twisting his sheets, twisting through bloated bodies in his dreams. Women with fish tails, thrashing. He had to untangle his legs from the winding sheets in the dark and straighten the bedclothes. Sometimes when he got out of bed he wasn't sure that he'd got out of his dream. The walls were somewhere within reach, they were black mirrors at the edge of his mind. He reached out for the walls but never turned on the bedside lamp. It was a game he played with himself. Almost gleeful. Except he never smiled because the dark was a test, it was dread country. The dark was his night-time woods.

With no moon. Unless his clock was the moon. He was serious about his big old round-faced clock, ticking *tock tock tock* and serious about the things he could do well in the dark woods. He could find his cowboy boots. He could piss in his toilet and never wet the floor. He thumbed his stupid cellphone. He hated his cellphone. Not that anybody ever called him. "The darkness and whoever's out there line dancing in the dark don't frighten this old shitkicker," he said aloud to himself, and he wondered why he never saw any old desperados sashay up out of the dark, their lips sad and tight, because he knew that down in the dark, on the other side of the clock there was a deep hollow place where they came from, their hearts as heavy as night because he knew that all the old desperados had been born to live lonely and to die lonely while waiting in the sunlight of High Noon and if they didn't end up nose first and dead in the dirt, then more than likely they'd end up their lives sitting wild in their sorrow in the sun looking for a noon train that was always late, sitting close by the long wooden legs of the lone water tower that cast a slim shadow toward the faraway blue hills, singing *Sa-loon, Sa-loon* into the badland winds. Tumbleweed winds that blew hot and dry and the thought of the winds that blew against the faces of all the old desperados left him soured and then enraged whenever he walked into the wind in the narrow downtown canyons staring at the tall glass bank towers at King and Queen Streets. The wind whistled between the towers. It was a whistle that had no words in it, no song, none that he could hear. A train whistle had words. A train had moaning words on the wind. He believed that he would never die till he heard a lonesome train whistle blow in the night and so he sometimes sat alone in the dark for hours without closing his eyes, angrily pitting himself against the dread, against the dark hollow behind the clock, waiting for the whistle, taunting death, listening, moaning, and singing *Don't cross him, don't boss him, he's wild in his sorrow*, bunkered down in his three small drywalled rooms in the basement of the stone house.

Before the house had been divided and rewired, it had been heated by a forced-air oil furnace, but now everything in the house was electrical. The cumbersome old furnace and the asbestos-wrapped pipes were gone, but all the air ducts were still in the walls, tunnels of tin sheeting that angled down between the floor joists to the furnace well. The wide air vents with their wrought iron gratings were still in the floors of the rooms. He sat in the dark in the square furnace well under the ducts and listened to voices from the upper ranges, to whispers, and cajoling, and laughter, and sometimes to screaming rage or whimpering. He'd heard a hundred voices in the dark and thought he'd heard almost everything there was to hear about love. "Yessir, I heard it all. Love's like a skeleton trying to dance itself out of its skin," he said to himself one night. He liked that. He'd seen a movie once where a boy who'd been left all alone in a prairie sod house had scared off outlaws in the night by painting a skeleton on one of his mother's dresses, his mother having been shot dead by a toothpick-chewing gunslinger, and he'd run out into the night wearing the dress straight at the outlaws, who rode away, terrified, and Albie could hear the boy's laughter as he waved his white bony arms after them in the dark exactly like Albie waved at cops as they drove through his crossing lane, waved at them with a curl to his lip.

Cops, he was sure, never heard music in the high branches. He believed it was possible some priests could hear sweet fiddling in the trees. He knew there was a priest who came into the Zanzibar every day late in the afternoon, dressed in slacks and a sweatshirt, furtive and hoping no one would recognize him, and there was fiddle music in the priest's eyes. Priests fascinated him. Priests in black. Crows. Sad lonely crows in whiteface. Or doves who'd dyed themselves in mourning dress, lonesome doves who knew how to stand tall and calm and benign at the end of the steel and glass world as it collapsed in on itself, crying, whispering and crying, like all the voices in the stone house that collapsed in on him as he sat in his chair, voices that tunneled in on Albie in the furnace room, down through the air ducts and into the long spells of silence in the cellar when all he heard was the ticking of the big alarm clock he kept on a table in front of his chair. The clock had a luminous round face, and as he sat hunkered forward in the dark to listen with his eyes open, he sometimes saw a smile on the clock's face. There were blasting wires attached to the clock. And the first floor, back and front, had been wired, too, through the ducts and the old floor vents. "There's standard time and daylight savings time. This is bomb time," he said and laughed to himself, alert suddenly to an anxious voice in the duct from the second floor. It was a woman who seemed to have a different man in her bed every night and her moaning cries came down the shaft and swirled around his head in the empty furnace well where he sat in a maroon leather easy chair. Her moaning aroused him, but he never masturbated in the dark. He'd always done that in the light, with the television blaring, alive to himself in his fingertips, but now that his mother had come to live with him he didn't do it at all.

~ 4 ~

Back on his ninth birthday, as he'd blown out the candles on a round Dollar Store cake, his mother, Emma Rose, had told him that he had no father, not a father anyone knew by name. "There was a man who you are the seed of but I have no idea who he is, and neither does he." She wasn't even sure what town Albie had been conceived in. "It's not that I was fast into the bed, I'm just an inch short in the memory, that's all. And besides, there's no point worrying," she said. "The world's full of worrywarts, and warts'll pester your skin, pester your mind." She had bright blue eyes and a pouting bruised mouth. She had a strong grip. She could break a walnut in the squeeze of her right hand. She'd given Albie her hands. Big-boned and a big middle knuckle. As a teenage girl, she'd wanted to go on the stage and had joined a dancing troupe, but she had never been light on her feet. Her feet were too big. She thought her feet were beautifully shaped, like the feet she saw on stone statues in the museum. Long sculpted toes. Still, they were too big. She'd been fired, but because she had several sequined costumes in her Samsonite suitcase, she'd persisted, hung in, and managed to travel the small mining-town Bingo and Big Top show circuit keeping the company of a knife-thrower named Mike Doov, and she'd been billed as Mike's Emma Rose. To steady his nerves, he'd snorted cocaine and said the rosary while she drove them from town to town.

At a miners' fundraising pageant, he had pinned her hand to the wall in the basement of St. Barabbas' Church in the copper mining town of South Porcupine. She said she'd felt no pain in the palm of her hand; instead, she felt it was like a trapdoor that had sprung open, as if the earth had broken apart, leaving her hanging over the gap, by her hand. Through the years her scar sometimes opened, and her palm bled. She was sure there was a reason for that, sure that her hand had a memory all its own of the knife, but the doctors at Mount Sinai Hospital said there was no reason. None. They were firm. "Hands don't think," they said. "Neither do some people," she said, "no matter how many scars they got." She'd quit Doov the knife-thrower and had worked for two years as a hostess out on the airport hotel strip, at Dade's, a dude trucker saloon that had a huge blackjack boot bolted to the peak of the roof and chrome hubcaps wired to the backs of chairs around the bar, but she'd finally been fired after finding two bar-rel-chested men, the chef and the bouncer, whacking each other off behind a Wonder Wizard pinball machine. She'd laughed and yelled *TILT TILT* and then had put a quarter in the machine and begun to bang away at the flippers. "Don't nobody forgive you for laughing at them, so they fired me, but it didn't matter," she said, "because some guy had already pulled down the night shade beside my bed and he'd whispered sweet nothings in my ear. Nothing. Nothing. Nothing. I had a weakness for wise guys."

She'd got pregnant, had never once thought about an abor-tion, and had passed her confinement quietly, working the phone for a bookmaker in a hairdressing salon until Albie was born in Grace Hospital, the Salvation Army wing. She said the horse that had won the third race while she was lying there in labour was called Fox On The Prowl and the first word she'd heard anyone say in the delivery room was, "Jesus." She had taken that as a sign. She was not exactly sure of what, but just a kind of blessing over his head. Albie insisted that he could remember the first word he'd heard from her: it was *Sa-loon. Sa-loon.* She laughed and said his memories were lunatic. "It must have been salon," she said, because that's where she'd worked, in the hairdressing salon, and because after all she'd taken no drink and known no men all through her pregnancy.

Then, once she'd weaned Albie, she'd travelled for several months with a man who sold aluminum siding and storm windows, leaving Albie in a foster home until she'd been hired on as the supervisor of a lakefront assembly line, spray-gunning lead finish onto the plug-end of television tubes. She liked being a supervisor. After six years, all the workers were warned that their lungs and innards were probably clogging up with lead poison. She'd lived at the time with Albie in a small studio flat but was sleeping on weekends with the divorced owner of another factory and so she went to work for him in his peanut plant, keeping the traffic and tonnage books on all the burlap sacks that were stuffed with unshelled peanuts. It was a dry musty building of tall ceilings and old windows with panes of marbled glass. She'd liked the quiet in the old building, and the bent light. She'd worked there for years, long after she'd stopped sleeping with the owner, and as long as Albie could remember, she'd had the smell of dust from peanut shells in her hair. He smelled it when she hugged him and she'd never stopped hugging him, not even when he'd turned 20 and come home sick-drunk, crouched over in the morning with the dry heaves, and not even when he'd come out of night court that evening wearing his turquoise cufflinks that he'd bought, blinded by the ceiling glare of the fluorescent strip lighting in the mustard-yellow hall, GUILTY, but then, not long after that, he'd gotten the job as caretaker to the stone house, the caretaker also being the rent collector for the dozen rooms and small flats, and she had fallen down the loading elevator shaft at the factory. "I didn't have no time to say *oops*," she said, "so I just yelled *SHIT* and fell."

After nearly a year in hospital, strapped to wheels and pulleys, "just splayed out like a fool spider caught in my own web," she'd said she would gladly come to live with Albie in the three rooms in the basement, giving him her small disability pension. He decided her money would pay for their monthly whisky bill. He liked whisky. Old Crow or any bourbon. He lifted a glass of bourbon to her health and heard himself say, "From here on in, home base is the basement." He was often surprised hearing himself say things that he hadn't planned to say. Afterwards, she sat all day in the basement in a wheelchair, sitting hunched forward, two spit curls stuck down on her forehead, turning on the computer he'd bought her because everybody was supposed to have a computer but she didn't really know what to do with it and he didn't know how to tell her how to use it so it pretty much sat there staring at her ear while she bobbed her head like a seasoned old boxer as she watched television, talking back to the talk shows. "You see those suckers on CNN they don't think a thing through to what they're supposed to be thinking, they just yell over each other," she yelled at Albie, and then she tilted her head coyly to the side and said, "This is fine, I never before felt so fine with you, Albie."

Every night and every morning for nearly three years, he'd wrapped a tartan mohair blanket around her limp legs and he'd carried her in and out of what had been his waterbed in his bedroom, settling her into the wheelchair, where she sat surrounded by broad-leafed rubber plants, popping caramels into her mouth, or exercising with the Ladies Trim Torso dumb-bells she'd ordered from a late-night infomercial, pushing them straight up in the air, and sometimes he thought she looked like a fugitive from the law practicing to surrender at gunpoint. One night, as she was about to lift the dumb-bells, he pretended to fast draw, slapping his hand off his thigh. "Bam," he yelled, pointing his finger at her. "Bam, my ass," she muttered, and then he heard low whisky laughter and he saw the desperado step out of the room's long narrow shadows, whispering to Albie, "You're a horse's ass. That's your mom you just shot." He said nothing. She slumped and dozed and then fell soundly asleep. Albie picked her up and carried her to the bedroom, but she began to whimper and whinge as he tucked her into the waterbed and so he sang to her from the foot of the bed:

Love is like a dyin ember,
till only memories remain,
and through the ages I'll remember
blue eyes cryin in the rain...

He slept on a fold-out sofa bed under the broad dark leaves of the rubber plants, and every morning he made her breakfast of toast and low cholesterol Egg Beaters that were good for the heart. "Because we don't want no fat around the heart. Lean and mean is what we want," he said, and then he laced up his yellow work boots and took care of the big old house, vacuuming the dimly lit hallways, making sure the Tough-Tuft wall-to-wall broadloom was carefully tacked down so that no one could trip on a loose corner and sue the landlord, and he changed dead light bulbs, replacing them with special long-lasting LED bulbs he bought from the Crippled Civilians' Society, and he fixed cracked walls with Polyfilla and semi-gloss paint that he'd mix to the right colour himself. He liked painting walls. Very few things gave him as much satisfaction as the smooth unblemished sheen of a newly painted, wet wall seen by the light of a bare 100-watt bulb. Sometimes, he'd decide to change the colour of a flat when a roomer moved out just so he could paint the walls. If it was necessary, he'd use a roller but he preferred a brush, and he kept several expensive camel's hairbrushes in a turn-of-the-century glass-doored cabinet in the furnace room. He never let anyone handle his brushes. Not even Emma Rose. Emma Rose had never been in the furnace room.

5

On sunlit and warm Sundays, Albie took Emma Rose by taxi down to the harbour docks and then by ferry across the city harbour to Ward's Island and Hanlan's Point and back. Otherwise, she sat in the basement flat and watched television all day. "You mark my word, TV is time travel," she said. "It's me and Spock, the eyes and pointy little ears of the world belong to us. And we're gonna find R2-D2 if it kills us." She watched All-Star wrestling in the morning, giggling as a bellowing hulk with pink hair wearing a rhinestone bow-tie slammed a fat bulbous bonzo in black studded boots to the mat, both wrestlers snarling into the camera and yelling *kill, kill,* or she'd watch *The Price is Right* or a program about a doctor who squeezed people's carbuncles and pimples, or another program she'd found that was all about 600-pound women, hilariously sad, she thought, huge sacks of suet flat on their backs "looked after by these little guys who all got moustaches, what does that mean, Albie? Fat women and moustaches, there's so many thunder-thighs out there, how do those little guys get it done?" She smirked at herself. "Albie, Albie, can you believe this moron-looking woman," she cried with a grim look of satisfaction, "can you believe it?" – pumping her dumb-bells up and down, excited and breathing hard…*phum, phlum…phum, phlum*…till Albie said, "You're gonna get arm muscles like a piano mover." She grinned and switched channels, pointing the remote at the red eye in the television Wonder-Box as if it were a ZAP gun. "Albie, these days everybody's watching everybody, all them birdwatchers are out there and the night watchmen and the watchmakers, but you and me..." *Blippety-blip-blip. Pip-pip. Blip-blip.* Applause for *Wheel of Fortune.* Blip-blip. ... "You and me, we're the watch to end the night," she said, and then she blip-blipped back to *Wheel of Fortune*: "Can I have an N...?"

"No," Emma Rose cried. *Tk, tk, tk, tk, tk, tk, tk, tk, tk,* of the wheel: – *"Five hundred." – "Can I have a D...?"*

"No." – *"Yes, there is a D." – "Can I buy a vowel, an E." –* "There are three Es."

"Morons," hissed Emma Rose – *"I'd like to solve the puzzle."* – *"Go ahead." – "TOMORROW IS ANOTHER DAY." "Right, right, and that's worth six thousand, two hundred dollars."* "Albie," she said, as he peeled open a silver foil of Old Chum chewing tobacco and tucked a chaw into his cheek and picked up his STOP paddle, "Albie, don't you dare forget it, what that fellah says there, tomorrow is another day." He was getting ready to go out for the noon-hour crossing.

"Don't bet on it," he said.

"Bet on what?"

"On tomorrow showing up like you'd like it to."

"It'll be what you make it, Albie."

"In a pig's ass."

"Never mind no pigs now. I got no notion about pigs, and their asses, but I been thinking a lot about you Albie, I was thinking about you this morning."

"You was were you?"

"Yes I was."

"There's nothing to think about me."

"I was thinking about the child you were, a real off-the-wall child."

"I wasn't so off-the-wall."

"Yes you were, carrying on like a little old man who'd never had no childhood, and now that you're older there's something kinda like a child coming out in you."

"No child I ever knew," he said and laughed.

"Well, not exactly like a child."

"What then?"

"I don't know. Maybe your father."

"My father ain't nowhere."

"But I been dreaming him, he's been coming to me in my dreams every night now for six nights, he knocks on the door and there he is."

She shunted back and forth on the big grey rubber wheels of her wheelchair.

"So what's he look like?"

"I'm not sure. He ain't at all like my own father but he's got my father's face, except I'm sure he's your father, but I still can't exactly tell who he is."

"What's he want?"

"To come in out of the rain. He's standing in the rain, and it's sloshing down outside and you're standing behind him with water running down your face. I'm the only one who's not getting soaked in the rain, and his face is like soap that's been soaking in water, kind of separating and coming apart in pieces, what you'd maybe call a weathered face, a weathered face on a thin stick of a man who's all angles with a boy's smile, a big smile that's very obliging-like so you shouldn't ever know how hard-bitten he could be, but then his eyes lost me, they just let go of their hold

21

on me before I could read their expression and when I spoke out loud to him it was like when you wake up after falling asleep in front of the TV and there's only that great greeny blue screen saying you've lost the channel connection, how do you lose a channel connection I'd like to know, leaving you with a big nothing."

"And what was I doing?"

"What?"

"Where was I? Still standing in the rain?"

"I don't know. I didn't look."

"You didn't look."

"No."

"I'm no goddamn dummy," he said angrily. "I don't stand out in the rain for nobody. Not for your dreams or anybody else's." He closed the brass fasteners to his fluorescent red jacket and adjusted the white vest cords around his waist, making himself comfortable, tying the cords in a bow. *Sashay, sashay.* He was in his stocking feet. "You and your dreams and those people you watch on TV are the dickheads of the world who don't mean shit, and all them computer fuckers and politicians coming out of the arse-end of everything."

"Don't talk dirty to your mother."

"I'm not talking dirty. I'm talking facts."

"Yes you are, with your dick this and shit that."

"Jesus Christ, Momma. I'm 34 years old."

"Then act your age and speak nice."

"I do speak nice."

"Let me give you a piece of advice, Albie. Free. You make sure, no matter what you think's going on, you make sure that you always say good words, and then eat some honey, and that way you'll never get a sore throat."

"I don't get no sore throats."

"You will and you'll be sorry."

"I'm not sorry for nothing, Momma. That's what you don't understand. I ain't killed no one. I haven't done a damned thing to anybody yet to be sorry for."

"We've all done something to be sorry for," and she pounded her fists on the arms of the wheelchair. "I am good and darned sorry for a whole lot of things, things I can't do nothing about."

"Neither can I."

"Neither can you what?"

"Do anything about what's done, except look after you, which I do."

"Yes, you do Albie."

"And I look after this house, and I look after all the kids who cross the street with me every day. That's a whole lot of looking after."

"You just make darnn sure you look after yourself," she said, as she picked up the remote. "Don't you be a sap and a fool for nobody."

He closed his eyes. He saw drowning white-bellied fish. He was no fool, not for anyone. "Not even Jesus H. Christ had better fuck with me," he said to himself, welling up with anger, an anger that was always there inside him, an anger lying close like a low fog hugging the ground. "You want to know how come I'm angry sometimes, I'll tell you how come I'm pissed off," he'd told Emma Rose. "It's like I haven't been doing nothing all day, not since I got up and washed myself off real clean, but suddenly right there, when I look, I got all this dirt under my fingernails, black dirt that didn't come from nothing or nowhere but it's just there, black, and that's what it's like when I find myself mad as hell."

It was a rage that he had no release for and no root that he could put his finger on. It just seemed to rest in him until it was roused, like an angry twin hanging on inside him to his ribs. One night after drinking whisky he'd decided that this twin was called George. "Just plain George," he told his mother. "And you know how hard it is having a brother who don't say nothing, not a word. Speechless and dumb. You ain't deaf, George, but you're dumb and that's tough, man. That's hard. That's no fucking fun at all." Then he heard beyond any question the word *grief*. A sound like an echo inside his bones. *Grief.* He felt a terrible loss. It was always like this. Whenever he was full of rage he felt the veins in his neck swell and an ache all through his shoulders, and then he was quickly drained, as if he'd been sucked dry and left shrivelled, in a cold sweat. He heard the word *grief* again but he didn't know what he'd lost and didn't know what grief is, though he'd often stood facing into a mirror wondering why he alone seemed to hear sweet fiddles in the high bare branches of winter and why he had this dumb clinging child in his chest and also the memory that haunted him of a man with a raspy voice singing, "*Love*, O love, O careless love..." *Pip-pip. Blippety-blip-blip.* Flares of light, SOSs, channels flipping. He pulled on his boots, listening for a train whistle in the distance, in the foothills. Instead, he heard: *Every shitheel's got to stand tall for something.*

"Who said that?"

The grizzled desperado winked at him.

What?" Emma Rose said as she stopped channel-surfing, and locked in on the evangelical station, and sat bolt upright for the preachers. "Nobody said a word." She wiped her hand across her face. She liked to talk about God. She liked to talk about God and stick out her tongue. "You want to find God," she said, "you check out the list of missing persons. We should put up posters of Him in the post office...WANTED. DEAD OR ALIVE – GOD. Haw, the poor son-of-a-bitch probably don't even know He's wanted, stumbling around out there in space with his thumb in the air, hitching a ride from here to Moose Jaw and back. Amnesia, He's probably got amnesia, stunned like some animal from staring into too many headlights in the dark, because those headlights'll do it to you, you get lights in your head just like these pop-eyed TV motormouth preacher fools, they seen the light, too much light for me, right in their own goddamn heads." She chuckled, and then laughed and hooted and went Haw, haw, punching at the air as the TV preachers pounded their Bibles.

Albie loved her laughter, but seeing her in the nest of shawls in the chair, punching the empty air, upset him, the way her barbell weightlifting upset him, the way the black apples on the apple tree upset him, finding a fallen withered apple in the snow right where he was looking for a desperado's footprint, right where he'd seen two men standing the day before, standing there eating what looked like a dried fig taken from a side coat pocket stuffed with dry figs, but then he too suddenly laughed as a baby-faced blonde woman, her eyes bright with the beamish light of salvation under a beehive hairdo, appeared seated on a mangy old camel outside the walls of Jerusalem, the camel led by short reins into a heavy swell of orchestral violins by two smirking men in striped ankle-length skirts, the camel carrying her down the stony hillside *bumpety-bump, bump*, as she tried to lip-sync a hymn, lip-ping the air with *Twelve Gates to the City, Hallelujah*, and as her husband's pious squirrel face suddenly appeared superimposed over her bobbing hairdo, crying *Lord forgive us, we know what we do*, Emma Rose began to howl with laughter, so that Albie, who'd leaned forward, squinting, realized that not one but two old sun-tanned desperados were out there on the desert hillside, smirking, dressed up in long skirts, and Albie, snaking his eyes to slits so he could see their faces and their silver-tipped shitkicker cowboy boots sticking out from under the hems of their skirts, said to himself, *"Ain't they some kind of motherfucker,"* as she yelled, "Heal, heal," whamming the flat of her hand against the air as if she were hitting the top of some poor sinner's forehead, Bam! "You jess step up here and slope your head for Jesus, *Bam*, heal."

~ 6 ~

Back on his 12th birthday, just as he'd blown out the candles on his cake, she asked him if the men in her life, the friendly strangers, upset him, and he said, "No, I don't think about it, I think about me."

"That's good," she said, "you go on thinking about you, because in the long run, you is all you got."

At 13, when she asked again, he said, "No, I'm not upset."

At 14, he said, "No, nope."

At 15, he said, "No," as one of her lovers moved in and lived with them for two months, a sallow-faced man, Yuri, who had dark shadows that looked like old bruises under his deeply socketed eyes, eyes, as he slumped beneath the hanging kitchen lamp, that were dark as the ebony stone in his mother's big ring where Albie believed he saw slivers of light go swimming and then drown, and whenever Albie looked into Yuri's eyes he thought of a ring of ebony water and silver fish and drowning, though he had never been swimming in his life, and so he told Yuri while they were talking at the kitchen table that he knew he would never die by drowning because he would never make the mistake of going swimming, but Yuri smiled and said, "Never mind, we drown, you'll see, we drown in our own puddle."

"No I won't."

"Why won't you?"

"Because I dream about water and fish, but I never die in my dreams."

"What else do you dream about?"

"Dynamite."

"You ever seen dynamite explode?"

"Nope. Except in the movies," Albie said.

"But you see fish?"

"The dynamite'll blow up all the fish."

Yuri said that he'd spent a long time in a place where everything seemed to have blown up and come to an end, where everything was always night, where even at High Noon you saw ash that was just like pollen in the air and you saw the night in a man's eyes, and there in that place he'd learned that the very end of things could happen every day and over and over in a man's head until it became only a dull hum, and men forgot all about the end and never needed to know what the beginning was, because men could forget what they'd been through almost as fast as they could spit, and that's what he'd learned when he was a boy himself, just a little older than Albie, working in the camp, what was called a concentration camp, where he'd learned to concentrate, to think, and it had been a camp attached to a stone quarry, so he knew all about dynamite but he never dreamed about it.

"Why not?" Albie asked.

"Don't know."

"What do you dream about?"

"God. I try to concentrate on God."

"You ever see Him?"

"No. And I'm not sure I want to," Yuri said, laughing. "I might try to kill Him." Yuri repeated the word *concentrate* over and over when he talked about his life, and Albie discovered that he himself saw yellow, or rather, felt he was being invaded by yellow, when he heard the word, the yellow of pus as it broke out of a soft and almost healed wound, and he remembered Yuri as a hulking man who sat in a cold sweat of sadness at the kitchen table, a man thinking so hard his mouth hung open.

He also remembered Yuri wore cowboy boots and said he was Ukrainian, "What not very nice stupid English call *hunky*," and that he'd been put in the concentration camp to learn how to think because he'd gambled with a Jew, gambled the gold in the Jew's teeth against a loaf of bread. The Nazis had arrested him and the Jew because they said he'd tried to steal state treasures, since all Jewish teeth belonged to the state. "This was so crazy it made sense," Yuri said. "All laws are laws only because they make sense with such logic." The people had been brought into the camp on trains in boxcars and he'd been put to work, because he was so strong, with a Jewish labour gang, a Commando, who helped unload incoming Jews, leading them to the gas chambers. "Jews leading Jews, the blind leading the blind," he said, "and I was only Uke." This gang, because some had pouches stuffed with watches and diamonds that they collected from the incoming Jews, was called Canada. It was the Canada Commando, the dream Commando, so he'd always thought of himself as Canadian, and he'd dreamed of Canada, of western cowboys, and horses, and cowboy boots. After the war, he'd come to Canada, but he'd never gone out west. "I liked the picture shows better, the movies. In movies, there are no checkpoints. I am proud citizen of this new country, Movieland Canada." He wore brown, tooled-leather cowboy boots and he polished them every day, and on Saturday afternoons he took Albie to cowboy movies. "You know what it is for me that I like to see about American movies?"

he said, "when you take all gunfire away, there is only silence, and it is this silence that could kill you, kill you badly." He loved seedless mandarin oranges. He would eat one after another, piling up the torn peels on the kitchen table. It frightened Albie when Yuri sat, sometimes for hours, eating oranges and saying nothing, lost in silence. "But there is silence and then there is silence," Yuri said, "and the only silence you got to watch out for is the silence before the calm of the kill."

"Did you ever kill anybody?" Albie asked him.

"This is not what you need to know, for such a small boy, beginning."

"So what do I need to know?"

"That during the daytime when you look up, because there is so much sunlight, you don't see the stars. But at night, when the dark is darkest, this is when you see the stars."

Sometimes on the weekend Yuri would get up in the morning and say to Albie, "She's asleep. Your mother's still asleep."

Albie would go into the bedroom and look at her.

"She isn't sleeping. She's pretending."

"No she's not," Yuri said.

"Her eye is open."

"How do you know?"

"It's white. She's dead," Albie said.

"No she's not. She's sleeping."

It was always around 9 o'clock in the morning when they talked like this, and Yuri made thick black coffee and ate a mandarin orange and paced back and forth in the narrow front room, bumping into furniture, talking to himself, pointing to the window. Sometimes he'd go back to bed and kiss and bite Emma Rose. She'd shriek and bury her face in his neck. Yuri yelled that he was tired. "I am very strong, but I am tired." She'd get up and brush her hair, the brush thick with strands of hair, and soiled. If Albie came into the room, she'd close one eye.

"I'm only half-awake," she said.

"You look like you're awake to me," Albie said.

"I'm only pretending."

"Is Yuri asleep?"

"No. He's dead."

"No he's not," Albie said.

"How do you know?"

"Because he's in his bare feet."

"Of course, he's in bed."

"He told me that when he died, he'd die in bed with his boots on."

Then, one weekend Yuri packed his small leather suitcase with its wrap-around belts and told Albie that he would always send him postcards from wherever he went in the world but he would never see him again, because he and his mother Emma Rose had nothing to say anymore, and Emma Rose stood leaning against the door jamb looking tired, because they'd been up all night talking and talking until they had nothing left to say, so he took Albie downtown for the last time and bought him a pair of boots. Albie, who was almost 17, stared at himself in the mirror, and the cowboy boots with their high heels gave his angular body a lean line, and he liked being so much taller, and liked the look of himself in the mirror and the look of Yuri smiling in the mirror behind him. He'd never forgotten Yuri's eyes, the old bruises. One day, he realized that they were the same eyes as the eyes of the desperado who'd appeared at the end of his bed, eyes full of night wind and wilting flowers. Sometimes, when he took off his boots and was sitting in the furnace room, he felt the hollow behind the clock turn into a well of dark flowers and sometimes, when he attached the blasting cap wires to the timing device on the alarm clock and sat listening to the ticking, he saw Yuri's eyes in the face of the clock, his mouth hanging open, concentrating, and he heard Yuri's soundless laughter.

↜ 7 ↝

"Television," he said to Emma Rose, "don't mean dick. You and me, we watched those wars in some desert somewhere, day after day, explosions where already nothing is growing, explosions in the same stone houses and the sky green at night with streakers of light all night long, and we ended up watching a war we never saw, except dickheads are discussing it like they saw something in the pictures that weren't there. Shit, if they want real pictures, I got pictures. I got pictures they've never seen, moving in my mind all the time." He laughed and slapped his thigh. "But I ain't like one of those loonies you see on the street, talking out loud to themselves, their brains bungholed and all screwed up. No sir. And I ain't no preacher." He knew what he was talking about because he heard words from deep in the back of his mind, luminous words, as if they spoke from inside mirrors, like razor cuts of light that tattooed the inside walls of his skin so that he winced and slitted his eyes and stared straight ahead, his body taut, as if he were trying to focus, to concentrate, absorbing an intense aching awareness behind his eyes, and when he was sitting with Emma Rose watching the evangelicals and one of them said that *God saw all there was to see with the freshness of vision in which nothing was hid, a vision in which the waters parted*, he wondered if God wasn't in him, God's words, because out of nowhere, the dark waters at the back of his mind would part and he'd see with utter clarity a telephone pole, or a dragonfly, or a lampshade on the other side of the room, or a twilit gunslinger, and there'd be nothing else there but the pole, or the fly etched in the air, alone in itself, or when he was walking down the street he'd fasten on a crease in the face of a weathered old man, or an unlaced shoe, and wings, white wings, and flying fish, he saw flying fish, and sometimes he wondered why he never saw angel wings as he sang *Bird in the sky flying high flying high* but then in his heart he was sure that angels, though there was no question that they had once lived and flown and fought with each other in the sky, they were gone now. The sky was like an emptied cutout book, full of holes, with the angels that had once been there all scissored out. What people used to believe in was full of holes. He was sure of that. He was sure because he believed he could see everything that was actually there to be seen, though he had no clear idea what all the things he saw meant or why they were so intently and suddenly lodged in his eye or whether other people saw things in the same way. And he always heard that word *grief.*

It came like a whisper outside the window. Like a dry leaf or dead branch blown against the glass. It was a strange sound against a cellar window. He never tried to say the sound of the word. He had never tried to tell anyone, not even his mother, about the gift he had for hearing sounds and words or for seeing things, and as for any blind spots, as for the possibility that something might be there that he couldn't see, he didn't ever doubt his own eyes. Only the feeling of loss left him wondering, the pangs so acute that he could feel an invasion of yellow in his bones and he knew, without knowing why, that sorrow was yellow. "Yes, yellow," he said, brought to a halt by a wild and prickly burning under his skin. The pins and needles of sorrow, his body gone to sleep. The burning made him furious. He chewed on his fingernails. He began to hum *It takes a worried man to sing a worried song* but he had no words, the letters lost on the wind like torn paper. Or flying fish. Once, he'd gone to church because TV preachers said the lost words were there, *holy, holy, holy*, but he'd felt an awful lethargy and a sourness in the church because what he'd seen was not God but people hiding. Faces shut tight. Dark mirrors. Like the walls of his room at night. He decided church was a place where people felt good because they were supposed to be able to talk to God. But he didn't see God in their faces. God wasn't talking back to them. He saw pews full of people talking to themselves, all of them stern, just like the police were stern. He was sure the church was a comforting place for the police, because it was punishment that kept cops and priests in lockstep, but Albie didn't want to punish anyone. Cops punished people. They didn't care who they hurt. Or beat. He'd seen cops beat up kids, kids who talked back. Cops didn't care if they were wrong, or the judges were wrong. The bald-headed judge hadn't even looked up. Albie was sorry that he had ever wanted to be a cop. He was sure his nameless father – who might have been anything – had not been a cop, just like Albie was sure that he himself was no thief, because he had never intended to take the white Stetson hat on his birthday, and any damned fool could have seen that, but the judge hadn't bothered to look up, the judge had never seen him because the judge had never bothered to look. But Albie had seen the judge. He'd seen that the blue veins at his pale temples were too blue, and the skin of his neck, under his flushed face, was the white of a garden slug. When he'd left the courtroom that night, a policeman at the door had said, "Sorry," and Albie had said, "So am I, that man is dying."

∽ 8 ∾

As he hurried down the street, passing a row of lean red brick houses, his black jeans tucked into his black cowboy boots, he began to hum, a humming so sensual in his throat that if he held on to a deep note it eased the spasms of anger which wrenched him so much that he hacked for air. He hummed, trying not to step on the sidewalk cracks. He remembered a little rhyme-song his mother had sung: *Step on a crack and break your mother's back*, and he walked carefully, skip-stepping between cracks so that he seemed to be a light-hearted man out for a stroll, swinging his STOP sign, and as he walked he sang out loud to the two old desperados that he'd last seen dressed in long skirts leading a camel downhill outside Jerusalem, but now they were in black jeans and black shirts, dressed just like Albie. They kept stepping out arm-in-arm from behind trees in the morning shadows, tipping their hats. Nothing desperados did surprised him anymore, not since the morning he had seen the gunslinger with the wilting flowers in his eyes, beaming at him benevolently as he swung in the breeze, hanging by his neck from the branch of an old elm tree, another desperado beside him, and Albie had cried out, holding his sign in front of his face, but then when he had inched the STOP sign down and looked again, the hanged desperados were gone. The air was empty. "Maybe that's how angels used to appear and disappear," he decided, pretty sure that the desperados had swung into sight just to taunt him, to fill him with a melancholy that he'd only recently learned to turn to a bittersweetness by singing, indifferent to anyone who sneered or looked quizzically at him as he passed:

> *Nobody slides my friend,*
> *It's a truth on which*
> *You can depend.*
> *If you're living a lie*
> *It will eat you alive,*
> *And nobody slides my friend.*

He only got upset and nasty if someone barged up out of nowhere and stared at him, stared at the chaw of tobacco bulging in his cheek or stared at his cowboy boots and his fluorescent vest, someone who soured his song, making him break stride so that he squinted into the sun, his eyes full of the snake spit that comes from knowing what it's like to sit with morning whisky on your breath, rolling a cigarette on a hot, hot day, licking the flimsy pale paper, waiting for the noon train, singing:

> *Been looking through the dictionary*
> *For a word that's running through my mind.*
> *Though I like the sound of brother,*
> *I've been looking for another*
> *That nowhere in its pages do I find.*
> *Can it be that all its glories are forgotten*
> *And are buried in the language of the Greek?*
> *If it is, 'tis always buried in my memory*
> *As the first word that I heard my Mommy speak:*

Sa-loon! Sa-loon! Sa-loon!
It runs through my mind like a tune.
Now I can't stand café, and I hate cabaret,
But just mention saloon and my cares fade away
For it brings back a fond recollection
Of a little old low-ceilinged room
Of a bar, and a rail
And a dollar, and a pail...
Sa-loon! Sa-loon! Sa-loon!

As he got to the southeast corner of his crossing lane, he faced an Army-Navy War Surplus store. The window was cluttered with ammunition pouches, fold-up aluminum fry pans, flare guns, flack-jackets, and nylon pup tents. A big inflated yellow rubber life raft hung from a second-floor fire escape. As he stood on the corner, singing *Sa-loon* to himself, he saw a middle-aged man in front of the store. Though the sun was shining, the man was wearing a clear plastic raincoat and a red scarf, and he had a brown paper bag full of crushed soda crackers. He threw a fistful on to the sidewalk. There were five seagulls on the corner. "God-damn seagulls," Albie said. "We're goddamn five miles from water and we've got seagulls shitting all over the place and you're feeding them."

"No problem," the man said.

"It's a problem, I'm telling you, shit's a problem."

"So say it nice," the man said. "It won't hurt you to say it nice."

"In your face," Albie said, angrily slitting his eyes.

The man spun away and stared back into the surplus store window, saw himself, and touched his cheek. "There's nothing in my face," he said. *This guy's a real lunatic*, Albie thought, looking at his watch. Real. He was always acutely aware of the time. It was 11:50. The school children would be along in 10 minutes. Trying to ease down his anger, Albie walked to another doorway, a LOVECRAFT lingerie shop, the windows filled with black and red garter belts, sheer brassieres, lace panties and feathered pasties. A hand-lettered sign over a box said *Orange Flavoured Condoms*. He looked hard at the box, and saw a woman taking into her mouth a cock sheathed by a condom. Orange-flavoured rubber. He stood transfixed. *That*, he thought, wagging his sign at the window *is fucking insane*, unaware that the owner of the store, a woman standing inside the door, was scowling at him. She wore a lapel button that said *Safe Promiscuous Sex*. She waved Albie out of her doorway. He shrugged and went back to the corner, to the man with the paper bag, but the bag was now empty, and he had crushed it into a ball and was tossing it from hand to hand. The seagulls had flown to the other side of the street. Children were coming along the sidewalk. The man looked in the window glass again, then turned on Albie. "You're telling me I'm in your face?"

"I told you," Albie said, "you're in my face."

"You're telling me?"

"Right."

"You're telling *me*, you're telling *me*, on a public corner to get out of your face?" He backed away to the curb. "*Me*," he said, buttoning his plastic raincoat and stepping backward into the crossing lane.

"Don't go backwards," Albie yelled, afraid the man would get himself killed.

"Backwards? What're you talking about? The whole blessed world is backwards."

"Don't walk backwards," Albie said sternly.

"I can go anywhere, and I can walk any way I want," the man cried, "and you better believe it."

The man waited for an Acme Distilled Water truck to make a right turn and then hurried across the street. He threw his balled paper bag at the seagulls.

"I don't better believe nothing," Albie said, and turned and held out his arms to the cluster of laughing children who were hurrying toward him, and some were shouting, "Albie, Albie."

He lined the children up in a row, telling them to hold hands, and they all did except a girl with braids swirled into a crown on top of her head who was walking with her head down and talking into her cellphone, and Albie thought sternly, *Pay attention, you'll get killed and I'll get blamed like it's my fault*, and then he stepped out into traffic, holding his STOP sign high. He knew how to look hard-faced and dangerous at drivers who encroached on the crossing lane. He waved the children forward, shielding their bodies as he walked beside them to the other curb. A few weeks earlier, a boy had given him a St. Christopher medal, a gift from his mother, and another boy had sneered, "That Christopher ain't a saint no more, they kicked that jive-ass out of heaven." Albie didn't care. The boy, tugging at his sleeve, making him lean down, had whispered in his ear, "That's you. My mother says you're my St. Christopher." Albie was so moved he'd wanted to cry, and he'd attached the medal to a silver chain. He'd bought the chain from a skinhead girl who was selling stolen jewellery in the stripper saloon, the Zanzibar, and he'd double-looped the chain around the alarm clock so that the medal hung suspended in the middle of the clock face. One night, he suddenly knelt on one knee and said, "It's you and me," and he kissed the medal before going to sleep and he'd slept well and now he kissed the saint every night and blessed the children.

"You going to sing today, Albie?" one of the little girls asked.

"No, no. We're too late today."

"Aw, come on, Albie," the girl pleaded.

As he led the three girls across the road holding the STOP sign over his head, he let out a high-pitched nasal wail:

I'll always be with you
For as long as you please
For I am the forest
And you are the trees.

∾ 9 ∾

Albie sat in the furnace well in the maroon chair. The leather was dry and cracking. It had been his mother's chair in the Cabbagetown apartment they'd lived in for years, four rooms in an old frame house that had been torn down to make way for First Permanent Place, two glass insurance towers that the newspapers said gleamed like gold in the late afternoon sunset because the sheets of reflecting wall had been fired with gold dust when they were in the state of molten glass, great gleaming towers of hundreds of thousands of dollars of dust. Albie dreamed of gold dust, of panning for gold with sourdoughs along crystal clear riverbeds, crouched over cold water at the foot of a dark ravine, watching for bears and wolverines in a ditch as dark as the foot of the stairs in the cellar where his mother had made him stand as a child, reciting his arithmetic tables, and whenever he'd made a mistake, she'd bolted the cellar door and left him alone in the dark where he'd dreamed of water in the walls and of dark forests planted in the fields of his skin. He never died in his dreams. He was steadfast, like the dark rich soil behind the stone house at the bottom of the garden, soil that was alive with worms, and his chest heaved under the constriction of the roots of pine trees, and the birds in the trees sang from the branches and the more they sang the deeper the trees sent their roots into him, drilling down between his bones and throttling him, and desperately he tried to reach up and catch the birds, tried to wring their necks, to stop the throttling, but the birds flew away to nests hidden in his mother's hair, and when she cut her hair she clipped their wings so that they had to stay in the low branches of the trees, still singing, but only one incessant note. *Dark. Dark. Dark.* Emma Rose insisted now that she couldn't remember putting him down in the cellar. "I wouldn't abandon a child to the dark." He told her not to worry, he didn't mind remembering the cellar now because he'd learned that, except for the tunnels in his dreams, the quietest and safest place in the house was the cellar, in the dark, and he confessed that sometimes as a boy he'd deliberately tricked her by leaving out multiples – particularly sixes, he didn't like the look of sixes – so that he would seem stupid and be left alone to himself. He'd quickly learned to walk through the cluttered cellar without banging into boxes and rusted old garden tools. He'd become sure of himself in the dark. And now, sitting in his mother's chair, he cupped his bony hands before his face, spat quickly into the palms like he had done when he was a kid playing sandlot baseball, and he rubbed the saliva into his skin and settled back. His hands had a sure sticky feeling. He liked that feeling. "Six times six is 36," he said, and laughed. "I always knew that."

⁓ 10 ⁓

Four air ducts opened onto the empty furnace well. He had made hinged lids for the square ducts out of plywood covered with white acoustic tiles so that he could close off any sound he didn't want to hear from the rooms above, particularly the stronger, shriller voices from the first and second floors. Very little sound ever came down from the third floor where there was a small three-room flat with sloping ceilings. It had apparently been lived in for several years by three dwarfs who worked in the local carneys. The carneys had closed down. Now, a big, heavy-set man who was an ambulance driver lived there. *The man upstairs*, Albie called him. He had no idea what went on up there, or what the man was like, except that he shaved his head clean and performed what Albie thought were tai chi exercises in the backyard early on Sunday mornings (Emma Rose said he looked like a man wigwagging SOS signals in slow motion), but the rooms in the rest of the house often sent down so many overlapping voices and so much TV talk and music, that he slumped down in his chair and felt he was travelling a night-time road listening to an old car radio out in the country, the stations drifting in and out of his head.

He was excited and alert when someone new moved into the house and he'd take off his boots and settle in the leather chair and try to hone in on the new voice. He knew where each duct went in the walls. He'd made a map of all the ductwork and vents in the house when he was laying down the wiring and the caps, drawing the wiring through the ducts to the clock. Still, it sometimes took him a week to hear the new voice, to separate intonations. He didn't try to see the face, it was the voice he wanted to know. On his rent-collecting rounds, he was flustered and shuffled his feet when he looked into a face in a doorway and heard the voice, so flustered that the air in the doorway warped. It was like peering through flawed glass, the face and voice veering apart, and he was sure that the voice he heard in his head was much more real than the face in the doorway. He didn't trust the face just like he didn't trust the faces that appeared to his mother on television. "Tonight," she would say, "David Letterman appeared to me. He was very sweet tonight."

"He didn't appear to you."

"Sure he did."

"Only angels appear to people."

"Are you outta your mind? That's what stars do, that's why they're stars, they make appearances."

"They make movies, Momma."

"Right, they appear in movies."

"And they talk to you?"

"Who else are they talking to?"

"Each other. They don't know you from Adam."

"You know the trouble with you, Albie?"

"No."

"You got an unkind streak, you got an eye that likes to hurt."

"Yeah?"

"Yeah. You like to hurt, you like your own hurt."

"I like my own hurt?"

"Right, you're a loner who likes so much to be alone, like being alone is better than being with someone."

"I'm with you, I got you."

"I'm your mother Albie. I'm your mother, you don't got me."

"Whatever I got, I got, and I like it. I like it like that, I like it alone."

"You know the trouble with you Albie?"

"No, 'cause I got no trouble."

"I don't want to say what the trouble is because I don't want to hurt you."

"Say what you want to say."

"You think your ass is a star."

"I think my ass is a star…listen to you, listen to you talk, and I'm supposed to be the one who talks loose, and listen to you. My ass is a star, but I'll tell you something, since you think the stars talk to you, I'm talking to you, this here star is talking to you. These are dangerous times, very dangerous, and you got to be on your guard the whole time, otherwise the bogeyman'll get you. You remember the bogeyman, Momma. Sing ring around the bogeyman all fall down. You told me about the bogeyman. The whole world's full of bogeymen. Big shot bogeymen who'd just as soon break my balls as look at me. Except I see them coming. With all their knucklehead politician friends lying on television about how much they lie all the time. Now even all the clowns are bogeymen. I got myself bunkered and I'll blow them beyond kingdom come before they can whisper through the walls how sorry they are, and sad, you ever noticed that Momma, how sad angry people are? Even the bogeyman, I'll bet even the bogeyman is sad."

⤚ 11 ⤙

It was only voices emerging from the dark that could unnerve him, the intimacy of all the words he heard, not the love words or the moans of lovemaking, but he thought that hearing voices the way he did, so close, so intimate, without his own body being there in the room beside the voice, was probably like being inside a woman without her knowing it, as if somehow a man like him could do that, could have that wet inner intimacy without even touching, a warmth like early morning rain that broke open to him as painlessly as a flower breaks open, or shells, oyster shells or peanut shells, all breaking open, with the words that he heard popping out just like peanuts, and he laughed because that meant his mother had spent all her years counting up burlap bags of unshelled peanuts, unshelled words. Bags and bags of words that had never been opened, never heard. But he heard the wrangling arguments in the house, the weeping into the phone of a placating woman lying on the floor, her phone beside the grille, whispering *Oh I want I want and I'll do anything you want because I just want you to want me* that was like being with people inside the words they mouthed, and if it was true, like the TV preachers said, that God overheard every word in everyone's heart, then maybe God, when He dreamed, dreamed He was Albie, and the Holy Ghost was actually a cop, an undercover cop who whispered the word that got someone killed. But unlike the cops, he didn't go in for mug shots, he didn't try to fix words to a face, didn't want to hold what he'd heard against anyone. He just cradled up in the hollow of the well, humming to himself, wanting to wish the lonely old desperados in his world well before he said goodnight.

Sometimes, before he stumbled to bed, in the shank hours of the morning when he couldn't sleep, when the house was completely still, and when his rooms were silent except for the light snoring of Emma Rose, he sat on the edge of the sofa bed with his boots off – the toes of the empty boots always turned inward – and the silence seemed to contain, like a seed, the word that he thought would unlock a question he didn't know how to ask. No matter how wonderstruck he was at all he had heard coming down the air ducts, that unasked question always hung out there in the shadows and sometimes the question seemed to haul him forward, so that he sat on the edge of the mattress, wary and alert and even afraid. Sometimes he thought the answer to the unknown question must be the word he always heard, *grief.* He peeled open a foil of Old Chum and tucked a chaw in his cheek, trying to soothe himself. He listened for the train whistle, or more frightening, listened for someone who was going to speak directly to him through the ducts, a voice that was going to name his name, throttle him, and at first he thought that this desire to hear a voice he did not know, a desire filled with dread, was a punishment for putting his ear to the secrets in the walls in the house, but then, because he had hurt no one, because he had not even told his mother what he had heard in the darkness, because he had kept the dark words as holy as a priest could keep them, he decided that what he was really afraid of was hearing his father's voice. Perhaps his father was on a train, whistling, coming back for him, to kill him. Or be killed.

Ever since his mother had told him about her dream, he wondered when he would come in out of the rain and cold and hear from his father, too.

~ 12 ~

On Saturday afternoons, Albie went downtown to the Zanzibar, a strip saloon on Yonge Street that had silver stars stencilled on the black walls, a stage studded with flashing lights, and a glass shower stall on stage. At the back of the long narrow room, a blind old black man played the organ, rhythm and blues. Two huge wooden canary cages hung from the ceiling and naked girls danced in the cages. The barroom was crowded with working men and women hunched over round black Arborite tables, staring deadpan at girls dancing on the stage, and other girls sidled from table to table carrying shoebox-stands, charging $5 to shuffle on the box beside a table and strip, or $10 if they got up on the table and danced.

Albie always tried to sit at the same table. He liked the slouching indifference of the girls, their hard baby-doll faces. He drank draft beer with a jigger of tequila in the beer. This drink was called Colorado Cool Aid, from a song by Waylon Jennings, a song about a bully who liked to spit beer laced with tequila in people's ears and then one day the bully got his own ear razored off by a Mexican who handed him back his sliced ear with the attached sideburn and told him the next time he wanted to spit, to spit in his own ear. Albie laughed out loud whenever he thought of that song and he felt so good he paid one of the girls to dance on her shoebox, cupping her breasts, stroking herself, parting her legs and bending over, touching her toes, so that he could see her vagina.

One afternoon, a girl who had skinny thighs, bent over and held her ankles and said, looking at him upside down, "Ya wanna kiss this? Fifty bucks." He looked sternly at her, unblinking, offended. He wanted to be left alone to his own thoughts. She straightened up and spun around, her pubic hair shaved and trimmed to the shape of a black diamond. He looked up into her pale eyes, eyes drained of light, and turned away to the stage where another girl had stepped into the chrome-encased stall wearing only Lucite high-heeled shoes. She stood inside the glass walls soaping herself in a shower of water. The organist played "Night Train." Albie was aroused by her glistening pale body as she drew handfuls of white soapsuds up her thighs and between her legs. He felt the swell of an erection and leaning close to the table so that no one could see, he took hold of himself, feeling a rush, a connection with himself. The shoebox dancer bent over again, looked under the table, leered and said, "Gotcha." He was furious. She spread her legs, pulling her buttocks apart so that he could see the rosebud of her ass. He knew the girls called this the Moon Shot. He ignored her, staring at the girl in the shower stall, her breasts sloping with fullness. Then the water shut down in the shower stall and the blind organist stopped playing. The shoebox dancer said, "So what'll it be?" He ignored her. She picked up her box and went to another table. "Gotcha my ass," he said. "Don't nobody get me that easy."

A dancer wrapped in a sequined shawl and sitting with the owner, Horace the Hop (he had a gimpy leg), a woman, whose heavy-lidded eyes made her seem sensually sure of herself, stepped on to the stage. Albie hunched forward, unbelieving. He'd rented a second-floor room in the old stone house to her, and for a week he'd been listening, trying to find her voice in the air ducts. He'd only heard a distant crying and someone somewhere sitting close to a floor vent, muffled words, and there was no way to know if it was her. As she shimmied on stage, her body seemed swathed in sweat, sweat pearling on her breasts. She slipped off her black halter with a coy laugh that mocked shyness. She was high-breasted, almost boyish. Sweat ran down her throat, between her breasts. She seemed to be suffering some intense inner heat, but under the sheen of sweat her skin was pale and there was no strain in her face, only an amused wry smile. A bead of sweat on her left nipple caught the light, caught his eye, and then it fell as she spun slowly on the balls of her bare feet, her palms joined together over her head, her head thrown back as if in ecstasy, but then Albie saw that she was watching herself in the ceiling mirror, and her wry smile was for herself. The men in the front row had become silent and Horace the Hop looked around, wondering what was wrong. Even the girl was aware, despite the bass pedal swell of the organ, of a deadfall of silence over the front tables. She looked back, as if someone might be behind her.

A man with a bulging neck, and his fleshy mouth puckered, pointed and bawled out, "For Christ's sake, she's bleeding." Horace the Hop cursed. A hairline of blood had stained the girl's white sequined briefs, and it was widening. "Goddamn, that's disgusting," a woman sneered. Horace hobbled up the stairs, grabbed the bewildered girl by the wrist and hauled her down from the stage. The organist stopped playing and Horace snarled, "Tell that blind fucker to get back on the pedals." Albie, arms folded, holding his elbows, yelled into a sudden pocket of silence, "Hey, Hop, that's the only human goddamn thing that's ever happened in here." Albie was taken aback, shocked at the loudness of his own voice. The owner was, too. He knew Albie was a regular who kept to himself, and for a moment he paused, but then he pulled the dancer toward the dressing room door and a mulatto hurried up to the stage. Albie ordered another Colorado Cool Aid, but he felt sour and glum. He spat his last mouthful of beer back into the glass and went home. He was home two hours early. He unhooked the blasting wires.

Through the week, as he worked around the house, tacking new rubber treads to the stairs, digging up flower beds that were spongy as the last of the frost eased out of the earth, he wondered whether she'd heard him yell in the saloon and whether she had been hurt and ashamed. In the furnace well, listening for her voice, he dreamed of drying her body with heavy towels, drawing a white towel down the runnel of her backbone. As the days passed, he listened for her step on the stairs as he checked the electric radiator thermostats in the halls, turning them down, and he glued down a corner of battleship linoleum in the vestibule. Once, at twilight when he was carrying a ladder from the backyard, he caught a glimpse of her hurrying into the house with an armload of groceries. The landlord did not allow cooking in the small single rooms, and that evening, in his stocking feet Albie stole to the top of the second-floor stairs, to the corridor where her room was, and he smelled frying sausages that could only mean she had a hotplate in her room, a danger to the old wiring because only the three-room flats had been rewired for appliances. But he said nothing and turned and went quietly downstairs. His mother, squinting at him, slumped in her wheelchair. At last she said, "Albie, what's eating you? You got some kinda bother on your mind."

"Windows," he said. "We only got goddamn cellar windows that aren't like real windows, where you can look out and see what's going on, or at least see out on the lawn."

"It's raining out."

"I'd like to sit and watch the rain."

"We got the whole world to watch," she said and switched on the channel selector. An electric sizzle fanned out across the grey screen.

"You got to be kidding," he said as the *Evening News At Seven* came on and he hunkered down into the easy chair beside his mother, who said, "I don't kid about the news, Albie. No sir, news is what makes the world go BANG." She hoisted her Trim Torso dumb-bells...*phum...phlum...phum...phlum*... "That's because our whole friggin' world is on a short fuse," he said, as the newsreader reported that several thousand desert tribesmen, after random testing, showed tumors on their lungs from breathing in the smoke and ash from oil well fires that continued to burn out of control in the desert. "Surprisingly," the newsreader said, "doctors say their lungs look as if they'd been working as coal miners for 20 years, and there is, of course, no coal in the desert." Albie smiled. An old gunslinger's soot-covered face was superimposed on the screen, singing *with whisky and blood all around, not even the wind heard a sound, since nobody prayed my friend...*

"You know the first thing I wanted to know about you when you were born, Albie?"

"I don't know nothing of first things," he said and began to sing along *since nobody prayed my friend...*

"Whether you were left-handed."

"What'd you care about that for?"

"Because of what I always wondered."

"Which was?"

"Why God's got no left hand."

"You mean," *with whisky and blood all around* "you mean God's a gimp?"

"He's got no left hand to sit on."

"Only dumbheads sit on their hands."

"It's in the Book," she said *with blood all around...*

"So where's His left hand?

"The angels always sit on the right hand, right?"

"Right."

"It's the devil."

"What're you talking about?"

"His left hand" *since nobody prayed my friend* "is the devil. You know how hard for me it was to find out that you were left-handed?"

"This is stupid, Momma."

"Stupid to you, but not to me," *since nobody prayed* "it wasn't stupid to God," *my friend* "look what's happened."

"Where?"

"Look how godawful the news is."

"Yeah well, what they say is going on is not necessarily what's going on."

"You think they're saying it wrong?"

"Who says they're saying it right?"

"I say." *and not even the wind heard a sound.*

"Who're you?"

"Your mother okay?"

"It's not okay." *and nobody prayed* "Maybe you're wrong, too, okay? Why not?"

"Because the right people," she said, *with blood all around* "know the right things."

"The right people know shit."

"There you go."

"There I go what?"

"I'm talking 56 channels of how the world is whack-jobbing the world and bonehead saints are setting fire to themselves with gasoline and refugees are coming over all the borders like cluster flies and it turns out the stars in the sky are cluster bombs blowing the hell out of everywhere in the air and you're talking shit."

"You're talking TV talk," he said scornfully, and he stood up and yelled, full of defiance, at the soot-faced gunslinger, "And you, you're just some friggin' dead ghost, you're not my dad," and he buttoned his fluorescent crossing-guard vest, and then said with grim control to his bewildered mother, "You know what the last thing a man wants to do is?"

"No."

"The thing he does."

13

At the beginning of each month Mr. Timko came for the rent money, came and put it in his green leather pouch. Mr. Timko had shining pellet eyes and he always smiled, his heavy lower lip wet, and there was a tiny split in his lip. Albie thought it looked like an overcooked sausage. He liked spicy sausage, and he liked Mr. Timko. When Mr. Timko had hired Albie, he'd warned him, "I only vork for landlord. Anybody late vith rent, then no vay, no vay for dem, and if too many too often, then no vay for you. Vee understanding each other because I have understanding vit land-lord and he vit me same as vit you."

Albie kept careful accounts in a neat hand in a Dollar Store's *Date and Data* book. There were epigrams and quotes on each page for each date. He liked to see his trim rent figures lined up beside some true saying out of history. He had never been short on the rent, and he liked to think his book had its own precise historical order as he entered a final Saturday notation and read: "Some of them believe in the immortality of the soul, while others have only a presentiment of it, which, however, is not so very different; for they say that after their decease they will go to a place where they will sing, like crows, a song, it must be confessed, quite different from that of angels." *Samuel de Champlain, Voyages, 1618*. As he touched the lead pencil to the tip of his tongue and wrote PAID beside Room Six, he wondered who de Champlain was, and then he wondered why he'd written PAID.

He'd only paid for the rent on a room out of his own pocket twice before, and that was after roomers had skipped out in the middle of the night, leaving him responsible, something that he'd never explained to Mr. Timko. He never wanted to be held responsible, to explain. He didn't want to be held, period. That's why he liked strippers and hookers. It was an intimacy without really holding. Room Six was the dancer's room and he hadn't seen or talked to her face-to-face since the morning she'd moved in. Troubled, and feeling melancholy because it was a sombre rainy afternoon, Albie greeted Mr. Timko glumly, but the cheerful collector said, "Albie Starbach, dis is good day." He was smiling broadly. He had little teeth. "Dis is good day for you, for me, a day ven landlord says vell done, dat Starbach man does not steal from me, so give him raise, and a raise to you too Mr. Timko for finding such a man who don't steal." With great formality, Mr. Timko shook Albie's hand. Albie was taken aback: "The landlord?"

"Landlord, yes."

"That's great, that's great."

"Yes, is great."

"Mr. Timko..."

"Yes?"

"You don't mind my asking?"

"You ask. Ask avay."

"Who is he?"

"Who's to know?" Mr. Timko shrugged and tugged at his lower lip.

"You don't know?"

"I never see," Mr. Timko said. "Is all phone. His office is his phone in his pocket, to me, he is only number."

"A telephone number?"

"No, no, no," and Timko laughed loudly, as if Alble had just told a big joke, and then he pulled at his lower lip again, saying, "Corporation number. Ontario 672160. You look your cheque vat it says."

"That's the boss?"

"Dis is boss."

"Son-of-a-bitch."

Mr. Timko smiled. It was pouring rain, steady sheets of rain in a rising wind. He wasn't wearing a raincoat or carrying an umbrella. He said goodbye. He didn't run or hunch up his shoulders against the heavy rain. He went down the walk and strode along the pavement with a measured pace.

14

Albie was sure all the school children had crossed the road but in the late afternoon he waited as long as he could for stragglers. He had given himself 26 minutes to get home. Then he saw a child, a boy about nine years old with thick blond curling hair. The boy had a long-legged loping gait, and then Albie thought, *what an angel baby face this kid is*, until he looked into eyes so unflinching that Albie blinked.

"You're new," he said.

"Yes sir."

"Well, I'm Albie."

"I need to cross the road," the boy said. "Will you take me across the road?"

"You bet your sweet life," Albie said, holding up his STOP sign as he led the boy out into traffic. It was early rush hour and drivers honked their horns.

"What do they call you?" Albie asked.

"Sebastien."

"I never knew no kid named Sebastien."

"No? Neither did I."

They paused on the curb.

"Where do you go from here?" Albie asked.

"That way," the boy said, pointing toward a small tree-sheltered park and a street that was a cul-de-sac.

"See you tomorrow," Albie said.

"Yes sir," the boy said, and went down the street. He turned and waved, and Albie waved his paddle, the red fluorescent STOP catching the falling afternoon light.

Because he was late, he hurried along the sidewalk, folding his fluorescent vest under his arm, pausing only for a moment on the front porch steps to the stone house because he still hadn't seen the girl, but then he went into the house and down the narrow stairs to the tubular bar of light above the door to the furnace room. As he took hold of the doorknob, he heard his mother hacking heavily for air in his flat. *Jesus, maybe she's dying,* he thought as he yanked the furnace room door open, rushed to the alarm clock and pulled the wires out of the timer, and then ran into his flat, stopped, and stood dumfounded. Emma Rose was walking around the room on her hands, her bare limp legs waggling out of her underwear, and she was grinning at him upside down. He yelled at her, "Goddamn, you scared me half to death. I thought you were dead. If you're going to do that, then do it out on the street so I can sell tickets." She stood still on her hands; her face flushed from the blood rushing to her head.

"You don't want me to go for a walk, Albie, not even around the room?"

"For Chrissake, this is awful. This is a goddamn scream."

"This is the way it is, Albie."

"You're talking to me topsy-turvy, Momma," he said. "It don't have to be this way."

"It doesn't, eh?" She rolled her eyes. They disappeared up into her head. Then she reached forward with three hand-strides toward the wheelchair, paused, and somersaulted in mid-air, landing square in the wheelchair.

He gaped.

"Where the hell did you learn to do that?"

"You think I just pooch around watching television all day?" She touched her two spit curls and then slapped her hands on the arms of the wheelchair. "No sir, Emma Rose does not rest. But you take it too slow and easy, Albie. You worry me. I end up thinking about you all the time. Like you should have a woman. A woman. Why don't you have a woman, sitting alone in there in your dark room for all hours, doing what I wouldn't ask."

"You got a dirty mind, Momma," he said, and stepped into the alcove kitchen to turn on the microwave oven.

"I got a natural mind," she said.

"Natural nothing." She always ate supper early, so he slipped a Meal in a Bowl out of the freezer tray, a picture of green beans and fleshy-white pasta gleaming on the box.

"You're a nut and you know it," he said.

"I don't know no such thing."

"If you weren't a natural nut, Momma, I wouldn't love you."

She drew her mohair tartan shawl around her shoulders, stared straight at him, but said nothing, tucking the tail of her shawl under her knees.

"Do you want the TV?" he asked.

"Whatever you want."

"It's not what I want," he said, turning on the TV.

"Sure it is," she said.

"No it isn't."

"Yes, it is."

"I don't want dick," he said at the ping of the microwave oven. He brought her a segmented white plastic plate of baked lasagna and greyish green beans.

"I don't like to eat alone, it's no good," she said.

"Good food's good food."

"No it's not."

"It's too early to eat," he said. "I'm not hungry yet."

"It's not too early to talk."

"About what?"

"I can see you got a lot of stuff on your mind," she said, "I can tell."

"You can't tell nothing."

"Yes I can."

He turned up the sound, sheltering himself in the rising pitch of TV talk, Channel 37, CNN. He wanted to be alone to think, cocooned, because faces and sounds had been verging in on him for several days, creepy crawlie things, and he could feel their wing speed, like insects, like dragonfly angels flying in the dark, and he sat trying to shuffle his thoughts into some order, wondering if what she said was true, that the upper daylight air, the daylight blue, really was filled with those cluster-bomb stars about to explode in the coming night. Dread. He was full of dread. He didn't know how to describe it because he wasn't sure where it came from. It was like a weight that was swollen inside him rather than just being heavy. It was a swelling inside his skull that sometimes made him afraid, and angry at being afraid, wanting to lash out to get rid of the dread. He was also acutely aware of Emma Rose lifting a forkful of lasagna to her mouth, touching the lasagna to her lips, testing the heat while still watching him out of the corner of her eye, never letting him slump back and be alone, never giving him a moment alone though she seemed to be completely absorbed in badgering the man who was talking on television: "Bunk," she snarled, *at what simply has to be done, and what has to be done, as Solzhenitsyn says somewhere, is…there's an inevitable increment of victims...* "Bunk, it's all bunk, whatever he thinks he's saying," she cried, *whose homelessness is in the heart.* "Bunk. Bunk. These guys are all bunco artists, and the women are all so dumb their tits are in a trance. Do you hear that Albie?" and she banged his arm with her fist. "Do you hear that?"

"No."

"You don't?"

"Sure I hear it. Goddamn fucking noise."

"What do you think about what they're saying?"

"I'm not thinking about it at all. I try not to think about it, I try not to rot my brains, I get a bad smell when I listen to those shit-for-brain guys."

"The TV don't smell."

"What's increment mean?"

"How would I know?"

"Albie, I'm worried about you."

"Don't worry."

"Why not?"

"Momma, I thought you were dying, when I came home. I thought you were goddamn well dying for sure."

"I ain't about to die. I never was no quitter, I never led no lickspittle life," *but now what we are forced to face about those victims who survive* "because I got along with or without knife-throwers all my life," *is that they not only know nothing about other victims, but they don't care—*

He opened a pine cupboard on the wall beside the basement window-well, a narrow window that shed a damp grey light, and took a bottle of bourbon from the shelf, poured two drinks, turned the TV sound down so that there was only the pale silent flickering of faces, shrugged at his mother's quizzical look and dropped a Willie Nelson cassette into the tape deck. "He can't be no down-home country singer," Emma Rose had said. "I seen him on the TV and he wears his hair in pigtails, a little girl's pigtails." Albie stood behind her wheelchair, sipping whisky in the muted light of the TV shadows shifting on the broad leaves of her rubber plant and he began to sing, lifting the tape deck's silver sound lever up until he was wailing in the dark, staring down at her lifeless legs dangling out of her shawls and sweaters, his high-pitched cry hitched to Willie Nelson's:

> *Take the ribbon from your hair*
> *Shake it loose and let it fall,*
> *Play it soft against your skin*
> *Like the shadow on the wall.*

> *Come and lay down by my side,*
> *Till the early morning light,*
> *All I'm taking is your time,*
> *Help me make it through the night.*

> *Well I don't care who's right or wrong,*
> *And I don't try to understand,*
> *Let the devil take tomorrow*
> *For tonight I need a friend.*

She sat with her eyes closed, letting on that she was asleep, and Albie knew she was pretending because one eye was open slightly, a white slit, just like when she had pretended to sleep with Yuri, so he sat down beside her and leaned his head on her shoulder, acting like he was asleep, too. After a while, he tucked her shawl close to her throat and then, as if he'd been caught doing something too intimate and shameful – like the afternoon when he was a boy and his mother had caught him in his room wanking – he smiled sheepishly at an old grizzled desperado, a desperado who had a rope burn on his neck, a man whose face – the colour of gristle – had suddenly come up on the screen like a face coming up from underwater, and he was watching Albie with a knowing look, and Albie turned up the sound to hear what the old man was saying, but it wasn't a man he heard, it was a falsetto, singing:

> *Rise, Charlie, rise,*
> *Wipe your dirty eyes,*
> *Turn to the east,*
> *Turn to the west,*
> *Turn to the one*
> *You love the best,*
> *Go in and out the window...*

"Who the fuck is Charlie?" He didn't understand why the old desperado, singing to him in some strange childlike voice, was calling him Charlie. "Albie," he yelled, "Albie," and his mother, bolting upright in her chair, astonished at the anger in his voice, said very quietly, very carefully, "Why are you calling yourself, son? Why are you calling to yourself?"

~ 15 ~

On Sunday afternoons the island ferry was always crowded with women and children who wore rubber thong sandals and carried hampers, soccer balls, and six-packs of beer and wine coolers. The two-hour cruise in the harbour stopped at Ward's Island and Hanlan's Point. Albie and Emma Rose stayed onboard. They enjoyed the light on the waves. Sometimes, if there was a strong wind, he'd get a head cold. He didn't get head colds on shore but he did on the bay, so he had started wearing a cap. He didn't really think of it as a hat. He still refused to wear a hat. It was a cap that he had bought at the war surplus store on the corner of the crossing lane, a paratrooper's camouflage cap. Maybe, he thought, when I'm wearing this cap no one'll be able to see my head, not even Emma Rose, who wasn't at all worried about the wind, or where his head was hiding. She loved the sailboats and clapped her hands in the late afternoon when the water was crowded with boats sailing out along the concrete and stone breakwater past the tall pines of Hanlan's Point. "Handkerchiefs," she yelled. "If you were God you could blow your nose all day." She laughed out loud at her own joke, hunched forward in her wheelchair, her head over the rail, the handbrake clamped against a grey rubber wheel and a safety bolt jammed between the spokes. The rolling of the ferry soothed her, and it soothed Albie, too. He sprawled to the side on a bench behind her, one leg crossed over the other, an eye half-cocked on her while squinting sleepily into the sun.

Sunlight made him drowsy. That's how he had got his head cold. He had fallen asleep under a strong wind, misled by the heat of the sun, so he did not trust the sun and he kept a watch for rising wind. And he watched while she bawled out whatever was on her mind, eagerly taking the wind-spray in her face, rubbing and stroking the spray into her skin, and when she hollered to Albie as if no one else were standing close by, he yelled back, indifferent to anyone on either side of him, but still, in his bones, he knew it was wrong not to narrow his eyes and pay attention. He always paid attention on shore, but he liked to think that out on the water he could be free, free to be alone, because being out on the water was like being out in the wilderness, and in his mind's eye he could see the desert badlands being water, and himself standing on a shelf of stone over the badlands. But that was in his mind's eye. With his actual eye, he knew that they were never alone and eventually they talked less and less. It was easy to stay silent because of the soothing rocking of the ferry as it crossed the protected harbour, and one day when they had not spoken for nearly an hour, she suddenly lifted her right hand and curled and wiggled her fingers, joining the tips, as if she were throwing animal shadows on the wall of the sky, and, amused by herself, she turned to see if Albie had noticed, and he had and he made finger curl signs back to her, as if they were talking sign language. They laughed and signed and scowled and pondered, and then she signed at him rapidly, as if she were making a stern maternal point. He nodded contritely, looked like he was pouting, and closed his eyes, seeing animals on the walls of his eyes, panthers, a cheetah, and what he thought was a wolverine though he wasn't sure what a wolverine looked like, but he saw teeth, he was sure of the teeth. He was sure of the dread. He clenched his fists, full of resolve, braced himself for the worst, and then he opened his eyes, but saw only that his mother had drawn her shawl close to her throat and she was staring out over the water, looking very happy, peaceful, like she had seen a bird in the sky flying high, flying high. He sat for a long time with the heat of the sun on his face, snuffling and snoring though he thought he was alert and awake, his mind drifting, teasing him – now that the animals were gone – with glimpses of the girl in the Zanzibar, as if she were standing on her toes, on the water, naked, not dancing but standing still, discreet, the beads of sweat on her bare body exploding in the sun the way he'd seen water droplets landing on a hotplate explode. Detonations. He made little muffled explosion noises, *phugh, phugh*, expelling air out of his cheeks. A baby, sitting upright in a carriage that had been parked beside him while he dozed, watching him, went *phugh, phugh*. He opened his eyes. The child went *phugh, phugh*. "Mind your own business," Albie said. The child's mother said, "Oh, I thought you were deaf and dumb."

"I'm not deaf and dumb," he said, shaking his head, disgusted with himself, because he had decided to ensure a silence in which he could hide and rest by pretending for the rest of the ferry ride that he was handicapped and could only sign. "I'm not deaf and dumb, I'm just goddamn fucking dumb." He got up and went over to stand behind his mother, to lean on the back of her wheelchair, saying, "Let's get off for once, see what's what."

"Okay, I don't mind."

"I feel like I wanta kill somebody if I don't get off."

"Jesus, Albie."

"Jesus nothing. I just want to get off. Damn baby's drivin' me nuts."

"What'd the baby do?"

"Nothing."

"You just want to kill it?"

"Making fun of me."

"A baby can't make fun of you, Albie."

"The baby was making the same sound I was making, that's all, like it was in my mind, reading my mind."

"Nobody wants to read your mind, Albie."

"You know lots, but you don't know that," he said. "You don't know what they'd love to know, what we're all thinking."

"I think you make a lot of trouble in your own mind for yourself."

"You think I'm dumb."

"I think you think too much."

"I think like I got to think."

"Sometimes you don't got to think, that's what you got to learn, Albie. You don't got to think, you got to relax your mind."

The woman pushing the baby in the carriage edged up beside them as the docking ferry let down its bumpers and reversed engines, easing into the wharf at Ward's Island. "*Phugh, phugh,*" the baby said, staring up into Albie's eyes. "*Phugh, phugh.*" Albie glanced at the child, cocked his thumb and forefinger and pointed it at the child and said BANG and then laughed. He laughed very loudly. "See," he cried to Emma Rose, "he understands me, he knows exactly what to say, *phugh, phugh,*" and he leaned down and kissed the child's forehead and the mother was about to pull the carriage away but then thought better of it, smiling warily, saying to Emma Rose, "He be your son?"

∼ 16 ∼

As he sat alone in the evening hours in the furnace room he began to drink heavily, full of rancor and resentment at the whispers he heard in the ducts, yet he was even angrier if there was only silence, so angry he thought he would retch, he thought he would retch, and he thought that if he were a woman, if he could ever be a woman, he would find he was barren...and sometimes there were tinsel lines of glittering light in his eyes, and floaters – dark spots, like dust, like dead stardust, he thought, laughing out loud to himself, taking another drink straight from the bottle – watching the shadows in the dark of the window-well shape themselves into hollyhock flowers and then into a bird hung by the throat from a horn in the moon, the moon rolling back and forth like an illuminated crystal ball in a dark glass box. He stood up and felt limp and took a deep breath before going to the window, peering into the glass, shading his eyes, as if he were looking far into a distance. He shook his head, discouraged, and folded his arms and shifted his weight to one foot, and with one foot in the air he suddenly felt relaxed, he had taken a weight off his body. He smiled and was about to hop back and sink down into his armchair but stopped, afraid that his chair would not be there, that he had no place to rest, that he would never have a place to rest, and rather than take a chance at sitting down he reached out for the wall, still standing on one leg, balancing, as if he were on a dark peak, water behind him, water before, and he was happily fondling the stamens of a strange island flower. He realized that he had hold of himself. He looked around though he knew no one was there, not wanting to be seen fondling himself, and fell back into his chair. He took a long hard drink and felt that his chest was full of tiny enflamed roots, and so he took a deep calming breath and folded his knees up against his chest, embracing his legs, the roots, staring straight ahead, hearing a woman's voice, sweetly singing.

He knew it was not a voice coming down the ducts. It was not a voice in a room. It was a voice in his head. His head was a room. He tried hard to keep calm. He knew he had to keep calm. He couldn't hear words. It was just a voice. A sweetness. An excruciating sweetness. A woman's voice as sweet as the little boy Sebastien's face. He leapt up again and went to the window, stood on tiptoe as if he might be able to see the crossing lane, though he was several blocks away, and then he shuffled back to the chair, sat down, embraced his knees, looked up and saw in the dark a black tulip open like a parachute in the ceiling. As it drifted down to the floor he said, "Holy shit, I must be losing my fucking mind. That flower's booby-trapped, it's gonna kill itself." He closed his eyes. When he opened them, the parachute was gone. He smiled. "Safe," he said, as if he were an umpire at home plate, and took another drink, determined to finish the bottle and get out of the basement room, get away from the empty furnace well, the blank face of the big round clock, the arrowhead hands holding the St. Christopher medal. It was 2 in the morning. He staggered as quietly as he could out the door, hoping that he wouldn't wake his mother, going up the stairs to the second floor, feeling more and more exhilarated with each stair, as if he were travelling in the tunnel of his childhood dreams, escaping surveillance. He tried to draw air into his lungs as he knocked on her door and when she opened the door and saw him standing in the half-light, grinning, holding a fresh bottle of bourbon, he said, "Remember me? I thought you might like a drink, we gotta talk about the rent and all."

She was wearing a beige slip, no stockings, high heels, and no make-up. He was surprised at how pale her face was and surprised at her thin lips, lips like an incision, a tiny cut that he could feel, a paper cut, and he winced, but then quickly smiled, and she smiled. She had fine white teeth, and she waved him into the small yellow room, saying, "Sure, sure, you're the caretaker guy down in the cellar."

He stepped in, swaggering a little.

"You shoulda been down to see me last weekend, and a couple of weekends before that," he said. "The rent, right, you're supposed to leave off the rent, like if you intend to go on living here."

"Well, I had some hard weeks, you know," she said, smoothing her slip. "So what's your name anyway?"

"Albie."

"Albie who?"

"Albie Starbach."

"A'll be a son-of-a-bitch," she said, and laughed. She had a deep, throaty laugh, the laugh of an older woman. That's a laugh that's been used, he thought, and said, "That ain't so funny," peering into the black glass of the back window, as if he were looking to see if there was anyone on the garage roofs. But he wasn't looking for anyone, he was looking at himself in the dark glass. "I know the whole score," he said.

"What score?"

"What's goin' on."

"Yeah?"

"Yeah, like the world, the Zanzibar. Take your pick."

"Oh yeah."

"Yeah," and for a moment as he looked into her blue eyes he wondered if it could be possible that she hadn't seen him while she was dancing, when he had called out to her, though she had been staring straight at him. She put two glasses on a small table, and he poured drinks.

"Ellen's my name."

"Yeah, I know, I got it in my book, I got it from you."

"Yeah, right, right, I got my name in a few books." She lifted her chin, saying, "So you like dancing girls, eh?"

"I like watching you," he said, sitting on a straight-back, old kitchen chair. She sat with one leg crossed over the other on the edge of the small table, so that he could see the underside of her thigh. The covers on the single sleeping cot close to the window were rumpled. He wanted to fix her covers. He looked around. There were a lot of things he could fix in the room. Cracks in the wall plaster. Polyfilla. He heard a hard whisky laugh. It was one of the old desperados, the one with the brown broken teeth, eyeballing him from the other side of the glass. He said as sternly as he could inside his head so that only the desperado would hear him: "Fuck off outta there." Then he told her how hard it was keeping track of people in a rooming house. "People come and go, come and go. Like goddamn ghosts. Nobody sticks close to nothing anymore." He took another drink and wished that he could lie down. He wished that he could lie down on her cot and be cradled by her. He wanted to be comforted. He was bone-tired of being angry. The blood was tired of banging in his head. He was tired of his headaches. He took another drink from the bottle, his glass empty on the table beside her. He knew she was watching him. He could not remember how long she'd been watching him. He wanted to remember that. To be exact. To play Xs and Os with each moment. He closed his eyes for a second and before he could open them, he saw himself spinning on a giant nipple, God's nipple, with his paper wings suddenly on fire, since nobody prayed my friend, and he began to laugh. Jesus, he thought, I'm really losing it. He opened his eyes as fast as he could, saying, "Your mother ever seen you dance, I mean, a girl like you, where you from anyway?"

"Petawawa," she said. "Camp Petawawa and she's dead anyway, though she just didn't up and die. She died a long time. Took a long time. She stuck with dying longer than anything else in her whole life."

"Shit, I'm sorry," he said, and poured her another drink.

"Nothing to be sorry about."

"No?"

"She done okay for herself while she was still alive." She lit a cigarette and stood up. She had long legs and good ankles. "What do you do anyway, I mean aside from sitting down in the cellar?"

"Traffic guard."

"What?"

"Crosswalks, you know. I stop traffic."

"You mean if I made myself a little girl again, you'd walk me across a crosswalk?"

"Right. Right," he said eagerly.

"Except, right now I'm as old as my mother was when she had me so no chance of my being a little girl again."

"Yeah," he said, charmed by her openness. "I'd look after you. I sometimes look at them little kids, and I feel sorry, sorry 'cause

I figure someone must be treating their lives all shitty. That's what most people do, treat others shitty."

"Well," she said, as if her good sense of herself and her mother had been offended, "nothing's shitty about my life, no shit on my heel, I got along good with my mother."

"Me too," he said, reaching for her hand. "Me, too." She let him hold her hand for a moment. He could see the shadow line of the inside of her thighs under her slip. He was sure she was not wearing panties.

"Hell of a way to spend a Sunday, eh?" she said.

"Sunday's just the worst," he said. "Nothing to do."

"Not much."

"Fucking boredom's a bugger."

"We could pray," she said.

"Sure we could," he said. "I ain't said a prayer since I was a kid." He was wonderfully drunk, and at ease, and so loose that he felt unhinged from himself, free-floating, like the spots he'd seen in his eyes, that stardust, or like the guys he'd seen in TV commercials for beer, hang-gliding through the air on the wind. She was twisting the satin string of her slip, one hand on her hips, staring with an amused brazenness at him, as if she had realized how hungrily he was eyeing her.

"What you say your name was?" she said.

"Albie, it's Albie Starbach."

"Albie," she said, and dropped one shoulder, keeping a hand on her hip. "How do you like it, Albie?"

"Any old way, any old..." he whispered, "goddamn, you're so goddamn beautiful."

"Oh yeah," she laughed and spun slowly on the balls of her feet, "and I bet you wanta see my tits, eh?"

"Yeah," he said, "yeah."

"Do I got tits as good as your momma?"

"Naw, naw, you don't look nothing like my mother."

"She's got no tits?"

"No, she's got no legs."

"Gimme a break, man."

"No kidding."

"Gimme a fuckin' break," and turning away from him, looking over her shoulder, she said, "Takin' my clothes off don't bother me, you know."

"It don't bother me either."

"Why should I be bothered?"

"No reason."

"The only thing I don't like about stripping in the club is the dancing shoes I wear, they smell so bad at the end of each night, I got to buy new shoes all the time."

"You want dancing shoes. I'll buy you shoes," he said as she turned around, her breasts bare. She had small pink nipples. *Little girl nipples*, he thought, *with an old woman's voice.* He stared at her. She smiled and cupped her breasts.

"Taking my clothes off, see, it don't mean nothin' to me."

"No, no, why should it?" he said, edging forward on his chair.

"I like to be looked at," she said. "Men, women, don't make no difference to me."

"No. Me neither."

"Sometimes some of the women who come out to watch us in the club, I know they figure us for some kind of whores or secret dykes, they got these squinty little eyes, but when I dance I don't think like I'm naked, right, 'cause naked's my costume, you know what I mean, like right now, you think I'm next to naked, but I feel just like when I was a little girl and put on high heels for the first time and a man looked at me and I knew he didn't see no little girl legs, and that gave me pleasure, bein' a woman, 'cause there's nothing better than bein' a woman."

He slid off the chair on to his knees, an imploring look in his eyes, and as he reached toward her, he said, "I'd like to kiss you. I'd like to give you something really good, like really kiss you. You know."

She shied away, out of reach, his yearning gentleness making her wary, as if she sensed that his only chance for any intimacy with her was a selfless offering of himself for her pleasure, letting her have her pleasure alone.

"Yeah, I'd really like to kiss you," he said, nudging forward on his knees. She put her hands on her hips and spaced her legs, her calf muscles taut as she stood waiting in her high heels, her fingers gathering her slip, slowly running it up her thighs until he could see her black hair trimmed to a diamond, as all the dancers did, and for a moment he rested his head on her belly, smelling her skin in the folds of her slip, wanting to taste the smell of the woman, the damp earth of mushrooms and sweetened saltwater, and then as he sank lower, her hands were on his shoulders, pushing hard, and his head snapped down and then she disappeared out of his sight and he felt only a crushing hot, damp weight on his neck and blood rushing into his ears, realizing his shoulders were against her thighs and that she'd pushed his head through her legs and she'd spun around and was sitting on his neck, yelling, "Ride 'em cowboy," squeezing his neck so hard that he was gasping for breath, and she smacked his back, kicking her heels. "Ride that fuckin' cowboy…"

He struggled, gripping her ankles, moaning, "No, no." Then he screamed as if he were in pain, "Stop. Goddamn, stop, please stop." She swung off him and stationed herself against the wall away from the door. He stood up, tears in his eyes, blinded by humiliation, his lips quivering. "I wanted to kiss you," he said, stupefied. "I just wanted to do a little something for you." He stumbled toward the door, and as he went out, she cried savagely, "You think I'd let a guy like you do me for the fuckin' rent?" She slammed the door. He stood very still, stunned, listening to see if the slamming door had wakened anyone. He took off his shoes so that he'd be quiet in his stocking feet, and he hunkered down as he went along the hall, enraged, grinding his teeth, but thankful that the desperado had not stayed outside the window to see him. The house was still, except that he could hear a gentle *tock tock tock* like a metronome in the back of his head, a voice singing, that same voice, a sweetness so sweet he wanted to cry.

~ 17 ~

It was pouring rain. Albie was wearing a heavy oilskin rainslicker. The rain was so heavy there seemed to be a mist inside it. It was hard to see. All the cars had turned on their headlights. Albie's feet were soaking wet. He was worried that the toes of his cowboy boots might curl when the leather dried. There were large, deepening puddles of water at both curbs but he stepped through them, being very careful as he took the children through the traffic. There was such a water slick on the road that the cars cast an arcing spray. His trousers were soaked. Anyone walking in the distance seemed to be a shadow. He had always liked the cold chill of rainwater against his face, but everything, the trees, the telephone poles, the doors to stores, people, the children were underwater shadows. He said as he stood in the pelting rain, "I can't swim." He knew it did not make any sense and he laughed. But he was serious: he couldn't see: his mind felt full of swollen waters and his dreams of drowning fish: the rain was a flood of water in his eyes. He blinked. He blinked again. He was sure that he saw two shadows down the street, a man, a child, and for a minute he thought it might be his father in his mother's dream, hunched but not hurrying, a hand on the back of the child's neck, holding and then hauling the child up onto his toes, a small boy, a big man in a tent-like plastic raincoat, but it was the man with the bag of stale crackers who had stepped backwards into traffic, and the child, the boy with the angelic face, Sebastien, who – as they stopped in front of him – looked up into the rain, into Albie's face, and said, "My father," and for a moment Albie was rattled and confused because he thought the boy had meant that he was his father, but then he understood that the man in the raincoat was his father and Albie was appalled. He heard the word *grief*. A sound like an echo in his bones. He turned away but the man said loudly, "Watch yourself," and Albie turned back, unsure if it was a warning cry to him or an alert to the child or just a cry in the dark rain, so he took the child's hand and held up his STOP sign and said, "Come on, Sebastien," and stepped into the crosswalk. The child kept close to him. He was wearing yellow rubber boots, a yellow raincoat and rain hat. He did not look back nor did Albie. "That was my father," the child said. "Still is, I guess," Albie said. Cars had stopped, the headlights, blurred by the unrelenting rain, made their faces shine. When they got to the curb Albie looked back. The man was gone. "What's he do, your father?"

"I dunno."

"What d'you mean you don't know."

"He's looking for my mother. That's what he says he does."

"Where's she?"

"Don't know. She just wasn't there six months ago."

"So he's looking?"

"Says he's a private detective. I don't like him."

"Don't talk like that, not about your father."

"I don't want to be like him."

"Maybe not, but don't talk like that."

"Why not?"

"Because, that's all."

"No it's not."

"What?"

"That's not all. I want to be like you."

"Me?" Albie said in consternation, stepping back.

"Yeah, the way you look after kids, all the kids, me, that's neat."

"Jesus," Albie looked up, for fiddlers in the trees. He didn't know why he was looking for fiddlers. There was no music. He was flustered. "I got only nine or 10 minutes, I gave myself only 19 minutes..."

"What for?"

But Albie, turning, strode away, yelling back through the rain, "I'll see you tomorrow. Tomorrow there'll be time," hurrying home.

~ 18 ~

The next day, in the afternoon after school, Albie and the boy stood on the sidewalk. There were broken branches on the lawns, brought down by the weight of the rain, but the lawns were fresh and green, and so were the leaves on the trees. They were standing in strong sunlight, the boy smiling, holding Albie's hand.

"I left us some time to talk today," Albie said.

"Can I walk along?" Sebastien said.

"Sure. But don't hold my hand," Albie said firmly. "You don't hold my hand anywhere but when we're in the crosswalk."

The boy looked at him, narrowing his eyes, but then he shrugged, and they walked on down the street, Albie holding his STOP sign in his folded arms, the boy holding his hands behind his back, like a little old man.

"So you want to be just like me?" Albie said.

"Sure, why not?"

"Why not? Because no one's ever told me anything like that before."

"I wish I had cowboy boots like you, too."

"Oh yeah."

"Yeah, except my father says they're stupid. He doesn't think my yellow raincoat is stupid, but he says cowboys are stupid."

"He does, does he?"

"Yep."

"I know a couple of old guys who'd tie a tin can to his tail for talking like that."

"You know some real cowboys?"

"I've seen an old gunslinger or two," Albie said, smiling.

"No kidding. Where?"

"Around."

"Where?"

"I been around. They been around."

"You talk to them?"

"When I want to."

"What do they say, what do they say back?"

"Back?"

"When you talk to them?"

"They talk mostly about themselves, tell me about themselves, about what it's been like waiting for the noon train..."

"Yeah..."

They were standing by the porch stairs to the rooming house, beside the apple tree. He could hear fiddle music in the high branches. He took it as a sign, a good sign. He snaked his eyes and turned to face the house and the boy did, too.

"This is where I live," Albie said.

"Neat," the boy said, as Albie was asking, "You ever see some people?" He put his nervous hands in his pockets, "You ever see people that may not be there?"

"Sure."

"You sure?"

"Sure I'm sure. One day in the winter when it was all deep snow I saw four red noses on the lawn in the snow, and I thought there were four clowns lying down under the snow but when I told them to get up they didn't get up and when I went and picked up the noses they were just round, red sponge noses you put on your nose if you're playing clowns so I decided the clowns must have gone away under the snow…"

"Oh yeah?" and Albie led him up the walk and into the house, down to the furnace room, to the square well under the ducts. He unfastened the wires to the luminous clock. "You sit there," he said, "and I sit here. This is my room. My special room. Everything that I think special, I think in here."

Sebastien, on an old pine workbench, looked around the dry-walled room in wonder, peering into the shadows beyond the well.

"You're not scared," Albie said.

"Naw."

"Some kids'd be scared, coming down into an old furnace room."

"I got nothing to be scared of. Safe as a church." He smiled so sweetly at Albie that Albie wanted to kiss his forehead but stiffened instead and drew back into his big easy chair. "That's right," Albie said, "and don't ever forget it. With me, you got nothing to be scared of."

Suddenly, they heard a loud voice singing down through the air ducts…"You been gone 24 hours and that's 23 hours too long…" and Albie, tracking the sound in the map of his mind, leaped up and left the boy and hurried to the second floor, knocked on a door, didn't wait for an answer, and strode into the bedroom of a fat little black woman who was lying on her bed in her slip, her legs bent and spread. Albie went directly to the CD player sitting on the grate and turned it off, saying, loudly, firmly, "Don't play this thing sitting it on the grate and don't play it so loud," going back out the door before the astonished, embarrassed woman could say anything. When he got to the furnace room the boy said, "I heard you, heard you talking. Where were you?"

"Upstairs."

"What's upstairs?"

"Rooms. The rooms I look after."

"You look after the whole house?"

"Yep," saying "Yep" again as he closed off the ducts, latching the little doors and singing:

> and if anyone finds us
> let them all be forewarned
> that you are the thunder
> and I am the storm.

~ 19 ~

The boy came to the house almost every day and stayed for exactly an hour. Albie gave him one can of Coca-Cola every day, and only one, and he never let Sebastien stay for more than the hour, watching the clock carefully, and watching the dark behind the clock because he didn't want any desperados sneaking up on them behind the boy's back, surprising and frightening him. "No mistakes," he said to himself happily as he sat back in the chair and talked to the boy, about school, and about the different people who lived in the house, but mostly about the desperados, his desperados, and how old Sam McCabe, the one he'd first seen come through the tumbleweed at the end of his bed, the one who had come out from behind the tree, the one with the eyes full of wilted flowers, had told him how he used to ride into a town when he was young in the early evening, and you could look to the left and look to the right and pretty much trust what you saw as much as you trusted your own horse in those days, which was a lot, because without your horse, without the trust, you were lost, and it made life easier if there was some trust, though it was hard living in terms of the getting of food and all, but if you were a red-headed stranger it was easier to know where you were coming from back then and where you were going, back in the days when a man was his word, pretty much. And men looked each other in the eye, pretty much. Of course, some desperados did some bad things that left him with a troubling mind, like Billy

Bob Monroe who had the scar over his eye and sometimes showed up with Sam and one time for a joke he was out there hanging with Sam from a tree, and the boy asked, "Was he dead?" and Albie said, "No, no, it was a joke, just a joke on me to see if they could surprise me." But then he told Sebastien that he figured this was how angels appeared and disappeared in the Bible and people were always talking to angels, some of whom he knew were hard and couldn't be trusted, and so it was, he said, with Billy Bob. Billy Bob was a hard man to trust, and in fact, he wasn't too sure at all about Billy Bob because he was a man who just said, bold as brass, that he'd shot and killed, in his lifetime, two men, two men who, he said, deserved to die, and were – he said – found to be so deserving, deserving to die, by a sheriff, but Albie said that he didn't know whether to believe Billy Bob or not because old Sam always made a sour face when Billy Bob told that story, and one day Sam had come right out and whispered to him that Billy Bob had shot the sheriff, too, but it was impossible to tell if this was true because they were two old competitive proud men who poked fun at each other a lot and Sam often sang:

If you're living a lie
It will eat you alive
And nobody slides my friend

saying that all he and Billy Bob really wanted was to be left alone and left free to say what they wanted to say and go when they wanted to go, from town to town if they wanted to, and they didn't want anyone trying to take their guns from them for no good reason and there was never a good enough reason to take a man's gun, so they were living out what was left of their lives in towns where no one could find them because the towns were forgotten, lost forever except inside their own heads as they sat in the noon-time sun by the old water tower waiting for a train to take them on home...

The boy, sitting with his arms folded and one leg crossed over the other, staring at him from the shadows of the well, unblinking, left Albie disconcerted for a moment – worried that he was talking not to a child but to someone who, behind the wondering eyes, was wise and could take all his secrets and use them against him. But then the boy said, "I knew I was right when I wanted to be like you."

"Every now and then I get a postcard from this one," Albie said, and he showed the boy a small packet of greeting cards held together by a broad rubber band. He snapped the band off and flipped over the top card that was a photograph of a fish and he read aloud, "Follow the Madonna, She Doesn't Eat Meat."

"What's that mean?" the boy asked.

"I don't know. Sometimes desperados talk strange, like they're talking to themselves. That's all he ever says on the cards, things like that. He wanted to go west, all the real desperados do, but he never got there, not that I know of, not yet. He only got there in the movies. Bought me my first pair of cowboy boots, took me right downtown and bought them and then lit out of town. Couldn't stand being closed in, because he'd once been closed in in a big stockade, a camp, like there are always camps in wars. And what he loved was seedless oranges. Always ate an orange, 'cause he told me that what you love is what you can't have. And the worst silence is the silence before the calm of the kill. He told me that, too. And soap. He loved soap so much he said prayers over it... And what's awful is people like him were given numbers, so they were just never more than numbers, numbers given to them by people like my boss, whoever he is, the boss who owns this house, who is also just a number…but men like old Sam McCabe, as far as I can make out, they didn't put up with any of that stuff, they just shot the numbers out of everything every chance they got."

"Maybe my mother went out west, too," the boy said.

"Maybe," Albie said. "It's possible."

"I like to lie awake thinking of her out west."

"Well, if that's what you want maybe it's the way it is."

"If I say my prayers?"

"Prayers might be good. I used to say prayers, prayers for my father. I think my father, though I've never seen my father, I think he might be in the west, but he's coming this way though."

"He might meet my mother."

"He might."

"That'd be neat."

"Yeah, but if he's coming, he ain't stopping, and if your mother's going, I'll bet she'll be going on ahead."

"My father thinks she's right here."

"He does, does he?"

"Yep. That's why he's at it all the time, trying to find her."

"What's he gonna do if he finds her?"

"He doesn't say. I think he wants to hurt her. You want your father to come home?"

"Well, he's never been here so he can't come home, but I sometimes think or maybe I sometimes dream he's coming."

"To take you away?"

"I'm too big to get taken away. And my mother wouldn't take kindly to my leaving her."

"Where's your own mother?"

"Next door."

"Your mother?"

"Yep. She lives with me. She's sick. She's got no legs. Not so you'd notice."

"Can I see her?"

"Maybe."

"You love her even if she's got no legs?"

"Yep. You should always love your mother a lot."

"I do. Sometimes I sit at her dressing table and look at myself in the mirror like I'm seeing her, and sometimes I put on her lipstick and I am her the way I see her. And I talk to me like I'm her in her mirror."

"How d'you know what she's saying?"

"I know."

"What's she say?"

"She loves me."

Three days later Albie took Sebastien downtown and bought him a pair of tooled leather cowboy boots, made especially to his size. The next day, two policemen met Albie at the crosswalk. They were polite but stern and sour and cold.

"You Albie Starbach?"

"Yes."

"Instead of young Sebastien Bawden we're the ones who're gonna walk with you back to your house today. If you don't mind…"

"Sure I mind. So what?"

"That's right. It don't make no difference. Just trying to be polite."

They walked along the street. Albie was sure they were being shadowed by at least one of the desperados, but he didn't look back.

"So what's this all about?" Albie asked.

"It's not necessarily about anything," one of the cops said.

"On the other hand, it may be about everything," the other said.

"We were asked by the boy's father to have a talk with the boy."

"Yeah?" and Albie began to sweat. He could feel black mirrors at the edge of his mind. The trees were filling up with hats. "So you talked."

"You know what he said to us?"

"No."

"He said he loves you. He said he loves you because you're crazy, you really believe dead old cowboys talk to you. Now why would a kid like that love you?"

"He said that?"

"Sure."

"That I was crazy?"

"Aren't you, talking to dead cowboys? You really do that?"

"Talk's cheap."

"We don't care about the talk, we care about the boy, you and a child in your cellar, and all this love talk. What's that all about?"

"Nothing."

"He says it's everything. He tells his old man that he loves you, that his old man should be like you," one cop said.

"You like little boys?" the other cop asked, trying to sound casual but sounding sinister.

"Don't be disgusting," Albie said.

"It's not us who's disgusting."

"Look," and Albie stopped in front of the house, his arms folded, the STOP sign flat against his chest, feeling so wronged that he wanted to cry, as he said again, "Look, I look after kids. I take kids across the road…"

"To your little room in the cellar."

"Fuck you," Albie said.

"Don't talk like that to us," the cop, who smelled of Brut, said. Albie saw snake eyes, two little crap-out dots, in the cop's eyes. "Don't you ever talk to us like that, bonehead, or we'll stick your dick face so deep in the shit you won't be able to tell the roses from your asshole."

Albie felt so distraught, so disappointed at what he'd been told and so invaded by the cops, the actual physical smell and sound of them, that his legs were shaking, thinking he was going to collapse. Yet he was angry, rage welling up in his chest, in his lungs, and he drew in a sudden deep breath, gasping with his eyes wide open and his shoulders back so that the policemen, startled, stepped apart defensively. Albie knew he had only about eight minutes, maybe less, so he asked very abruptly but politely, "What's the day today?"

"The 19th," one cop said.

"Why?"

"So I figured," Albie said, and then he said, hoping that they would leave him alone so that he could hurry into the house, "Anything else, gentlemen?"

"No, not for the moment, but you'll hear from us."

~ 21 ~

He sat staring for a long time at the luminous white face of the alarm clock, listening to the heavy *tock tock tock*. He watched the hands with their arrowheads move. He counted the numbers on the face, backwards and forwards. He had made supper for his mother, but he had not been hungry himself. He had not been able to talk to her. She had wanted to talk about monarch butterflies, the beautiful butterflies she'd seen on television, how they had flown thousands of miles south to roost in one or two trees, millions of butterflies in a few trees, and someone had cut down the trees and the monarchs had fallen out of the air, their bodies settling around the tree stumps, piling up and covering the stumps, piling up heaps of dying, suffocating butterflies, all because some idiot had cut down a tree. Albie had stared at her. "What the fuck is she going on about?" he'd thought. She had wagged her finger at the TV. He'd wagged his fingers at her. She'd wagged back. "Holy shit, we're nuts," he had said to himself, making a small mound of white Reddi-Wip cream in her bowl of cherry Jell-O. He'd licked some Reddi-Wip from his fingers and then poured himself a Jack Daniels, and at last, after she'd asked, "Aren't you hungry, aren't you going to eat?" he'd said, "Follow the Madonna, she don't eat meat."

"What?"

"Never mind. I don't know what I'm talking about, I'm going across the hall."

He sat in the furnace room. He could feel time ticking in him, speeding up, *tick tick tick*, and because there was no sound in the air ducts, he thought, "I wonder where that ambulance man is, maybe out doing his tai chi," and he got up, rewired and timed the clock, and headed for the back door though he knew his mother, sitting trapped in her chair and left alone without explanation, would be thrashing her arms back and forth, upset and worried about him, but he couldn't explain anything to her. He couldn't explain anything to himself. He couldn't explain how he felt, except that he felt betrayed, deeply betrayed, and humiliated... he felt like he was a puke, a puke, a puke – he kept saying over and over – a puke at the hands of a jerk in a raincoat, and he was angry. He knew his anger. He could talk to his anger, it was somebody in him, it was George, his twin, a wild dwarf of a man who had settled into the right side of his ribcage, teeth like a slavering dog, leering, full of rage, Albie's rage, feeding and feeding off Albie's rage, getting fat, bloated, and suddenly Albie cried, "Jesus Christ, the little fucker's having a shit, he's taking a shit inside me, I can feel it," and Albie leapt out the back door of the house hoping he was a skeleton leaping out of his skin. He landed on his two feet. He knew he was still in his skin. He began to moan, a long low sorrowful moan, a moan that rode like a chill on the wind. It was a yellow wind but the chill soothed him, made his skin clammy though it was still warm out; it made him shiver, and he stopped moaning and said, "Never mind, I can think straight if I have to, fucking right I can," and he thrust his shoulders back like a soldier and he walked in a straight line to the back of the garden, looked at the dark house, dark except for one or two windows, and he decided he would wire the back of the house, too, that he had enough wiring and more than enough explosive, and he strode briskly in a straight line to the house, to the side alley, to the street. "What I'd really like to do is wire the fucking cop shop," he said out loud as he turned to go downtown, to Yonge Street, to the Zanzibar.

22

The club was not crowded. There were two paratroopers at the bar. He could tell they were paratroopers. He knew most of the military insignia. He had studied them in the war surplus store. They were dead drunk, trying to pop beer nuts into each other's open, gaping mouths. Nuts were bouncing off their cheeks and foreheads. Then, one threw a fistful of nuts at the girl dancing in the shower stall. The nuts rattled off the glass walls and the paratroopers roared with laughter. Albie thought, Fucking jerks. The bouncer, a bull-necked man who wore a black T-shirt with the arms cut out and black gloves with silver studs in the knuckles, went up to the troopers, put his hand on their backs as if he were being friendly and said, "You guys may think you're tough soldiers but I'll bite your ears off before you get off your stools." Albie laughed. He knew the bouncer had just been convicted in court and had paid a fine for biting the earlobe off the ear of a Hell's Angel biker. He'd read about it in the papers. The bouncer had swallowed the earlobe. He had said in court, "If he wants his earlobe, he can look for it in my shit." One of the troopers turned, going to throw a punch. The bouncer whipped their two heads together with a slam of skull to skull. It sounded like a pistol shot in the night. The two troopers toppled off their stools to the floor. Albie felt a strange exhilaration. He despised stupid soldiers. He despised stupid cops. He'd seen soldiers before, yelling and drinking and vomiting as if they couldn't care less that there really was an enemy out there. "Pukes," Albie called them, staring at their half-conscious and jerking bodies, blood in their crew-cuts, and he laughed, thinking he'd like to jerk off over them, he'd like to see every boy he'd gone to school with lined up and jerking off over them. "Weird, man," he said as he went to the back of the room, back beside the stall where the blind black organist played, back where there was a row of little round-topped tables in front of fake plush chairs.

He sat down. It was a dimly lit section set aside for lap danc-ing. There was an old man in the chair nearest to him and a girl was straddled across his legs, naked, rubbing her thighs against his. He was giggling, giggling and bobbing his head. "What's so funny?" she snarled, "what's so fucking funny?" He kept giggling and trying to touch himself. She kept slapping his hand away. Girls who were caught whacking a customer off were fired. The girls could rub against a man, but the man could not touch a girl, or himself. It was the law, the liquor licensing law. Albie stared through the brown light and smoke. She was coming down from the stand. He signalled the cruising hostess. "Her, I want her," he said. "Thirty bucks," the hostess said, took the money and went and stopped the girl, who shrugged, and turned toward Albie. For a moment, he felt upset in his stomach…not so much sick, as empty, as if he had been pumped empty. He watched her walking toward him in her high heels, her panties, bare breasted. She had not come to see him about the rent. There was nothing he could do about that. There was nothing he could do about her, not now, not with what was going on, not with the cops wanting to jump on his head and shit in his hair. If he threw her out, she might go to the landlord and say that he had tried to get her to fuck for the rent. What could he say? He had been in the room, on his knees. He had seen films of pilgrims, people on their knees, walking on their knees toward holy waters. No one was going to listen to him now, not even if he walked on his knees. No one, not with a couple of cops prowling around asking about little boys. He was stuck with her, and stuck with the rent. He had not done anything, not a thing, but he felt the walls closing in on him, the girl, the cops closing in. *You think your ass is a star. I'll pay, okay...for now,* he thought, smiling grimly as she hesitated, startled to see that it was him, and then, with a wink she stepped out of her panties and straddled his thighs. She moved her buttocks slowly against him to the rumbling beat of the organ. "Hello again," he said very quietly. She didn't answer, staring at a spot on the wall above his head. "You don't need to talk," he said, leaning close to her breasts, whispering, "I didn't pay for you to talk. I don't want you to talk." He had an erection and he tilted his hips, pushing up against her through his trousers. "Congratulations," she said without looking at him. He took a deep breath, inhaling her sweat and a musky perfume she was wearing. "I can pay for you anytime," he said. He loved the sheen of the sweat on her body, wanting to feel it on his cheek, the wet softness of her skin, and he clenched his fists and said again, "Any time," feeling her push and grind down on him, as if she could break him, hurt him, not moving to the beat of the music, but grinding, and she flattened her hands against the wall for leverage, leaning so that her breasts were so close that they brushed his face. He closed his eyes. He saw animals. Teeth. Smelling her. He could taste the smell of her. Apples and asparagus, he didn't know why he thought of that. He hated asparagus. It was a taste that filled him with a sadness, a yearning, but he didn't know what he wanted. *"What the fuck do I want?"* as he pushed his hard-on up against her again, feeling bitter and so disappointed because he had only wanted to give her pleasure in her room. He heard the words *give* and *grief*. He opened his eyes. She was moving faster and harder on his body. He flicked out his tongue and tasted her sweat, tasting smoke and salt, knowing that she was trying to make him come in his trousers, trying to humiliate him as he felt the urging rush in his loins. He didn't care. He touched her nipple with his tongue, tip to tip. She stiffened, surprised. He suddenly took her nipple in his mouth, held it hard, sucking in. "Ow," she said, and hit him on the neck with the heel of her left hand. He held on, sucking, taking more of her nipple into his mouth. "Ow, Jesus," she cried, and chopped at his head. He let go, her body springing back but before she could get her balance, before she could get up off his hips, cupping her sore breast, he grabbed her by the shoulders, grim with a hard triumphant anger, and he pulled her toward him and bit her shoulder, not breaking the skin, but taking the skin between his teeth, clamping down and then letting go, leaving his mark. Howling with shock and pain, she whirled away and ran toward the front of the room but the owner Horace the Hop and the bouncer were already running toward Albie, who sat very still, his head down, trying to go blank as fast as he could so that whatever was going to happen to him would happen before he knew it. He heard the bouncer, who he remembered had a snake tattooed on his upper arm, yell, "I'm gonna break you fucking in half," but when it didn't happen right away, he came out of his blankness and looked up and saw that the owner had a hand on the bouncer's arm, right by the snake. "How come you?" he asked, as Albie shook his head, shrugging, saying, "I don't know. I don't know...Look, just lemme leave, don't hurt me, I'll never come back..." The bouncer reached for him and lifted him out of his chair but Horace the Hop said, "Never mind, Ronnie… let him go, he'll go quiet."

"You saw what he did to Ellen?" the bouncer said, aggrieved, and whining at the owner.

"What about it?" Horace the Hop said.

Albie stepped quickly between the tables of staring men and the standing naked girls, trying not bang into anything, trying to shift his hips as smoothly as he could between tables, relieved – and almost unable to believe that he wasn't going to get beaten up, thinking *Snake Eyes* – as someone swung open the front door, holding it open for him, and "At least she didn't make me come. No sir," as he stepped through the door, heading north toward home, suddenly in quick stride with one of the desperados. "No sir, she did not do that."

~ 23 ~

He was standing close to the crosswalk curb, in the sunlight, his hands linked, holding the STOP sign, sure that all the children had come through the lane after lunch and now were safe in their school chairs, all except Sebastien – he hadn't seen him for more than a week – and Albie knew that that did not bode well, but the sun felt surprisingly good on his face. He didn't feel drowsy at all. He took a deep breath as he heard a voice say, "Mr. Starbach?"

"Yes."

There was a portly, heavy-jowled man standing beside him.

"Mr. Starbach, I'm Mr. Cather, the school trustee. I hope we can do this smoothly, Mr. Starbach, but in light of the police and all, questioning the children about you, you see, I mean, we can't have that kind of suspicion and consternation, can we, you can understand that, so while all of what's going on is going on, we've decided, the school trustees that is, that it's better that you don't do the job you're doing here at the crosswalk, for the sake of the children, you can understand that, what with how confused the children and all must be about you…"

Mr. Cather had reached out, attempting to take Albie's STOP sign, but Albie had stepped sideways, almost backing into the LOVECRAFT doorway, holding it behind him, edging away, saying grimly, "Okay, okay, I understand, I get it, okay…" catching out of the corner of his eye: FRENCH TICKLERS AT HALF PRICE.

103

He hurried home. He was sure that he had seen Sebastien far off in the distance but he couldn't be sure if his eyes were playing tricks on him, and he went straight into the furnace room to his chair in the well. He closed his eyes, trying to find a place of calm in his mind. *Tougher than leather.* Salt was tougher than leather, tougher than love. The boy, standing in the distance, was salt. Suddenly he leapt up, yanking the wires attached to the clock. "Jesus," he said, sitting down, "I'm losing it. Kill my goddamn self if I'm not careful." He took a deep breath, leaned back and stared at the ceiling, realizing that the sound lids for the air ducts were still in place. He opened them and listened. Not a sound. The house seemed to be completely empty. *"That stripper bitch is probably still asleep,"* but then he forgot about her almost immediately. *"I know the score, six times six is 36, minus two is 34"* but how was he going to hide all this from his mother, how would he ever tell her that he'd brought a little boy to his furnace room? Day after day? He broke into a sweat. And what if the police went to Timko, or even to his boss, whoever 672160 was, because the police could find out things like who a number was, and what if Timko had to fire him and had to tell him to get out? What would he do then? What would he do with his mother? "How the fuck're we supposed to live if they do that?" he cried. He opened up his *Date and Data* book. Everyone was paid up except the girl. He wrote PAID beside her name and read the entry note for the date, May 21: "On May 21, we set out with a west wind and sailed north as far as the Isle of Birds, which was completely surrounded by drifting ice…The great auks are as large as geese, black and white in colour, with a beak like a crow…our longboats were loaded with them in less than half an hour…" *Jacques Cartier, Voyages, 1534*. He touched the lead pencil to the tip of his tongue. He had never heard of an auk. He knew the awk. Awk was how he felt, it was what people said in comic books when everything was turning to rat shit in their lives. "Awk, awk," he said, and then, feeling better, he began to sing, *Bird in the sky flying high, flying high.* He got suddenly calm. He didn't know how that had happened, how he had found the place in his head, but he had. He had found a piece of the sky in his head. He took a deep breath. Then he thought of the bay, of the water, he and his mother, their laughter, making finger signs. He wondered if it was as silent underwater as people said it was, as silent as the sky. He didn't know. He couldn't fly, he couldn't swim. He'd never really been underwater anywhere, not long enough to listen. He found it hard to believe that there was no noise, that the fish didn't hear things, all those scaly minds talking, and what did the sun look like from underwater? Like it was drowning? And what did people look like to a bird? He knew a song from school:

> *If I had the wings of an angel*
> *And the arse of a big black crow,*
> *I'd fly over these prison walls*
> *And shit on the people below...*

No one he knew had ever talked to him about these things although his mother had once told him about how we had all millions of years ago come up out of the sea. Tiny little things looking like snake heads with nubbly legs, but it was hard for him to imagine the old unshaven desperados being nothing more than a tiny head on nubbly legs. The closest the desperados had ever got to water, he figured, was the water tower by the railroad line. They had never had anything to say about water. They had little or nothing at all to say these days. The desperados seemed to be hiding out. He hadn't seen one since he'd fled from the bar and even then that desperado had broken stride and had crossed the street and walked parallel to him all the way home, as if he were walking shotgun for him, watching out for him, and then he had ducked down a laneway that ran off the empty street near the house and since then he hadn't seen anyone and Albie began to sing:

I'm going to leave here running
because walking's most too slow...

He felt a lot better, much calmer. He had hardly said a word in days to Emma Rose. He went into the apartment. She was wrapped in her shawls, watching television, the *Springer* show. Fat warpheads in the afternoon. This guy Springer, and the audience yelling, *Jer-ry Jer-ry Jer-ry*, as some woman who looks like she was born and bred at a Texaco truck stop says that the father of her child isn't the guy she's living with but is the guy's brother and Springer says he's got the proof of who the father is in his pocket but he's not going to tell anybody until they have enough time, all three of them, to try to punch each other out, *phumpf phumpf phumpf*, nothing but air punches, and screaming and, bouncers pulling them apart and Emma Rose screaming along like life is a scream-along, which made him laugh and say, "What a lousy life."

"It's the way life is," she said.

"On the other hand, maybe it's all fake," Albie said.

"Naw, naw, it's real. It's right there."

"But he could pay them to pretend all those things."

"Naw, this is no pretend, Albie. You and me, we pretend about things, Albie, but this is no pretend."

"I don't pretend," he said.

"You been pretending nothing's bothering your mind," she said.

"Nothing is."

"Nothing?"

"Nope," he said. "Anyway, it's all nothing."

"Don't seem like it to me," she said.

"It don't, eh?"

"Nope," she said. "What we're into here is forever."

"Two nopes make a dope," he said.

"Haw. Haw."

Jerry Springer had appeared on the screen again, so Albie said, "Well, got to go," and he picked up his fluorescent vest and STOP sign and went out. He stood on the front walk beside the apple tree and buttoned on his vest and then wondered what to do, where to go, walking up the street toward the crosswalk. There was somebody already there, somebody standing by the curb holding a sign. "Holy shit," he said. "Holy fucking shit." He turned and walked the other way, for about eight blocks. One of the desperados, Billy Bob – whom he hadn't seen for a month – stepped out from behind a maple tree, wagging his arm, like a railroad wigwag, pointing Albie out into the traffic and Albie held up his sign, STOP, and the traffic stopped though there were no crosswalk lines painted on the roadway. *Sashay, sashay.* Albie waved at Billy Bob, yelling, "Come on, come on, then," but the desperado stepped back behind the tree. A car honked just as an old woman stepped into the stoppage and crossed over and as she passed Albie she said, "Thanks, sonny," and he said, "Think nothing of it." After half an hour of stopping traffic he went home.

He went back to the same place for the rest of the week, three times every day. Whenever anyone wanted to cross, he stopped the cars and took them across. A couple of people recognized him from the school crosswalk, but no one asked why he wasn't there, or why he was stopping traffic where there was no giant white X painted on the pavement. They smiled at him, glad to see him, glad to cross safely. The cars stopped. No one objected. No one honked. He was efficient at helping elderly people. Every day the same little old woman he had helped on the first afternoon came by, pulling a little wire shopping cart on two wheels. She always said, "Thanks, sonny," and he always said, smiling happily, "Think nothing of it."

Then, at noon hour of the second Tuesday, he held up the sign realizing that he was staring through a windshield at the ambulance driver, the man upstairs from the third floor in the house. The driver was staring back at him, and checking to see if there were any crosswalk signs, and after Albie let the traffic move, the ambulance pulled over to the curb and the driver got out and waved him over. Albie stopped two cars and went across the road.

"What you doing, man?" the driver asked.

"Nothing."

"No way," he said laughing and rubbing his clean-shaven head. "There is no crosswalk here."

"I know," Albie said, wondering whether he was rubbing his head for luck.

"But you're stopping traffic."

"Yeah."

"Fantastic," the driver said.

"Right."

Then the driver looked at him and said, "You okay, I mean, you're okay?"

"Sure."

"Well, it's not everybody who decides to spend the day stopping traffic any old place."

"It's not any old place."

"No?"

"It's my place."

"Right. Right, I shoulda figured. Well, listen, it's great. Love it," and he laughed again and got into the ambulance and then said through the open window, "You're okay, you're not in trouble?"

"No."

"Well, like, if you feel in trouble gimme a holler."

"Naw, there's no trouble."

"Right. There never is," and the ambulance man drove off, but as Albie watched him go he felt himself welling up with panic, with the usual dread, afraid for himself, for everyone, "Big trouble, fucking big trouble," and when the ambulance was about a hundred yards away he yelled, "Deep shit, man," and he stood in the centre of the road and started waving the STOP sign back and forth and up and down but the ambulance kept on going and Albie was afraid that he was about to cry, he felt so sorry for himself, and bewildered, sure that the ambulance man must have seen him in his rear-view mirror, and he said, "He probably thought I was doing my own tai chi stuff." He laughed wryly and looked to both sides of the road. There was no one there. Not Sam and not Billy Bob. "The sons-of-bitches," he thought. "They pick their own time and place."

∼ 24 ∼

On Thursday, he got a phone call from Mr. Timko, asking if they could meet on the next Saturday, at the house in the morning. Albie, trying to sound jovial and relaxed on the phone, said, "I guess the boss wants to give me a bigger job, eh?" Mr. Timko just laughed and hung up. Albie was rattled. He walked back and forth in the furnace room. "This is it," he said, pounding a fist into the palm of his open hand. "This is fucking it." He waited for the dark waters in the back of his mind to part. They didn't part. He went out into the backyard. There was no one there. There were no lights in the windows on the third floor. There was no music in the trees. "This is it." He took an angry swing into the empty air. He hauled a triple-section ladder from the garden shed, a roll of wiring, his tool case, and a sack of Amex. He ran the wires up the corner drainpipes and secured the explosives under the eaves. "Top and bottom, back and front," he said, and put the ladder away.

Inside the apartment, his mother said, "Let's ride the ferry this Saturday, if it's nice, in the afternoon, okay Albie?" He put his arms around her, "Sure, sure, babe." She held on to his arms for a moment. "It gets more and more lonely down here, Albie, you know that? Lonely as hell, when you get right down to it."

"Well, you got me, Momma."

"Sure, but I can't have you forever. I don't want you forever. I want you to have a life, Albie, a real life, without me."

"So, what're you going to do?"

"What I've always done. Look after me. I can look after me."

"Sure. Sure."

"Don't sure sure me."

"Right," and he wiggled his fingers at her and she wiggled hers back and they both burst into laughter and she cried, "TILT" and he said, "Saturday for sure," as he picked up his STOP sign and went out singing, *Don't cross him don't boss him he's wild in his sorrow...*

~ 25 ~

At around 1:30 in the afternoon, as he was about to go home, he saw a man on the other side of the street, a man who was watching him. The man had been there for about 10 minutes. He had a camera. Then, without waiting for Albie to stop traffic, he crossed the road, sidestepping the moving cars. He had bushy hair, a moustache, and a big easy smile. He walked right up to Albie. "Hi," he said, "Tom Sloper's the name. I wanna talk to you if it's okay."

"Okay for what?"

"For the paper. I'm a reporter, a photographer, for the *SUN*."

"I ain't no tassel twirling Sunshine Girl."

"Naw, we heard about you. It's a great little story. Stopping traffic, helping people all day just for the sake of helping them, it's a terrific human interest story. It'll cheer our readers up."

"You want to take my picture?"

"And know all about you. I want to know all about you. Everybody'll want to know about you, it'll do you good, too."

"Jesus Christ," Albie cried, and turned on his heel and hurried down the street. When he was far enough away he turned and yelled, "You take a fucking picture of me and I'll kill you."

"I already did," the photographer yelled, waving his camera over his head, smiling happily.

Albie got home and told his mother that he was sick, that it must be something like a flu, his head was pounding and he wanted to bring up but he couldn't, he had the dry heaves, so he wasn't going anywhere, not for a day at least, he was taking Friday off, and what he needed to do was sit in the dark, in the quiet, he needed to calm the nerves in his stomach. "Keep calm no matter what," he said, as he watched her hoist her Trim Torso dumb-bells…*phum…phlum…phum…*

"You should try lifting weights, Albie," she said.

ᵔ 26 ᵔ

On Saturday morning, shortly before Mr. Timko was to arrive and just after Albie had made his morning attachment of the wires to the clock, there was a knock on the furnace room door. He had made up his mind to slip out to the corner 7-Eleven to buy the *SUN* to see if his picture was in the paper, so that if it was he could be ready for what Mr. Timko might have to say, when he heard the knock. He didn't bother to press the lever on top of the clock or move the alarm hand. He opened the door. It was the two cops. "Hello, Albie, mind if we come in?" one said, as he came in.

"Your mother told us you were here," the other said, holding a handkerchief. "She can really move in that chair, your mother."

"Yeah, nice woman, and this looks like a real nice room you got here, Albie."

"Yeah, well come on in," Albie said as tight-lipped as he could, falling back into his chair.

"Your mother says you're sick."

"Naw, I'm not sick."

"She trying to put us off?"

"She thinks I'm sick."

"Maybe you are," the cop, wiping his nose with his handkerchief, said.

"Very funny," Albie said.

"We're not here to be funny, Albie."

"Yeah, so what're you here for? You got a warrant?"

"Save that warrant shit for the movies, Albie. We're just here to talk, maybe more."

"So."

"So, we got a problem," and he blew his nose.

"Like what?"

"Like my allergies, like I got allergies to everything."

"Too bad," Albie said.

"Yeah meanwhile, we also got a very respectable father who wants to kill you, and we can't have that, can we?"

"So lock him up," Albie said.

"We make an arrest," the other cop said, snickering, "and it's gonna be his nose that we'll be arresting."

"What?"

"Him," the cop said, pointing at his partner. "It's his nose that's on the run," and he laughed loudly. He was wearing Old Spice. Albie wanted to ask him why he had switched from Brut to Old Spice but thought better of it. *Bird in the sky flying high, he sang to himself, bird in the sky...*

"Yeah, yeah," the snuffling cop said, "except we got this kid who says over and over he loves you, but he never did nothing with you down here."

"That's exactly right."

"Maybe it is. Maybe it's not," the cop said, his voice muffled behind his handkerchief. "I got a little experience with these things, you know. Maybe the kid's too scared to say what really happened..."

"Not likely..."

"Maybe you got so deep inside the kid's head he liked what went on here and he don't want to tell us that, maybe he really does love you..."

"Maybe."

"That's the way we look at it," and the cop blew his nose again, his eyes watering.

"Look at it any way you want, though if I was you I'd watch out for yourself. You look terrible."

"I do, Albie, I do."

"I'll bet."

"Don't bet, Albie, don't bet on nothing. Didn't your father ever tell you that, don't bet?"

"I got no father."

"You got a father complex?"

"What the hell is that?"

"You like little boys."

"Get off it."

"Get off what?"

"Get off me. You fucking ruined my goddamn job, they took my job, you know that, so now what're you gonna do?"

"Get to the bottom, Albie."

"There's no bottom. You got it all wrong."

"I tell you what, Albie," but the cop sneezed. They waited for him to blink and get his breath back.

"See, this is the mystery for me," the other cop said, "this is the thing that just don't fit. Why should a kid, a beautiful intelligent kid like that, why should he think he's in love with a skuzzball like you, a nothing little creep, eh? Now answer me that."

"You got all the answers, you answer it."

"No, no. That's the point. I don't have all the answers, and that's what really bugs me. Why you? The kid's got a wonderful father, why you?"

"The father's a nutcase," Albie said. "He feeds seagulls so they can shit all over the place, and he walks backwards into traffic."

"Yeah, yeah, you're a big-time authority on traffic. But I tell you what I figure. I figure the kid is never gonna break, he's never gonna tell us the truth. He's gonna protect you and protect you, you insidious little shit. You think I haven't dealt with guys like you before, goddamn misfits trying to fuck kids?"

"You're fucking crazy."

"Yeah, and Mona Lisa was a man."

"So what we think we're going to do, Albie," the watery-eyed cop said, muffling his mouth with his handkerchief again, "is we're gonna take you downtown, give you a taste."

"A what?"

"A taste. You get away with this one, okay. But you guys chasing sweet meat, you never quit. There'll be another, and we'll get you, and this is what it's going to taste like, a little time in the can, time behind bars."

"You can't do that."

"We can't, eh? You fucking well watch us."

"I got things I got to look out for today and tomorrow. Who's gonna look after my mother?"

"See, Albie, see what happens when you want to dick around, you want to molest kids."

"I didn't molest nobody, you're molesting me."

"Jesus Christ, listen to him…"

"Get what you're taking, Albie, and come quiet, don't cause no more trouble than there's gonna be."

Albie got out of his chair. He looked into the dark behind the clock. It was full of black tulips, but there was no one there, nobody. He said, "You want to play your game, go ahead, I don't got to take nothing. I go clean."

"Good, Albie, good."

"Sure."

He stepped between them, and then, when the cop blew his nose again, he reached out and touched the St. Christopher medal that was hanging over the clock's face and moved the alarm hand to 3 in the afternoon. "A stitch in time saves nine," he said, shrugging, and the cops looked at the old clock and shrugged, too, and then Albie said, "I'll just tell my mother I'm stepping out."

He leaned forward on one leg into the apartment, using the door to shield the cops from her sight, and said, "I'm just going out, Momma, don't worry about nothing, no problem. The two Dick Tracys were just looking for a place to put parking tickets. It's ferry time for sure."

He walked between the cops to the patrol car that was parked at the curb at the end of the walk. As one of the cops opened the back door, Albie said, almost in a whisper, his hand on the roof of the car, "You'll be sorry, Jesus H. Christ don't fuck with me," and he looked back at the house, a house he had done so much work on, a house that he thought of as his home – even if he had had to live at the bottom in the cellar – and then the whole house was awash in his eye in a yellow light and a surge of sadness and remorse and loss hit him and he turned and got into the car. The cop put his hand on top of Albie's head to protect him, "Watch your head." Albie saw that Mr. Timko was standing down the sidewalk, looking distressed, and Albie waved, crying, "Don't worry, don't worry Mr. Timko, just go home," as he ducked his head, laughing as he heard the word *grief* and said over and over again, huddled in the back seat of the car, staring at the bullet proof glass shield and steel grillwork between him and the two cops in the front seat, "Oh Jesus, Jesus, Jesus…"

~ 27 ~

"There's no charge for the room," the cop, who smelled of Old Spice, said, as he closed the police station cell door. Albie stood holding his trousers up with his hands. They had taken his belt and shoelaces. "And there's no charges, either. We're not charging you with nothing, Albie. So you stay here a few hours, and then we're sending you downtown, to Don Jail for the night, to hustler's row, you'll love it. After they hose you down for lice and go up your ass looking for little plastic bags, you'll spend a night with the boys. You'll love it. Educational. We're all for education, Albie. Just think of us like we're taking you safely to school." Albie didn't say a word. The other cop, who had taken a clean dry handkerchief from his desk on the way to the holding cells, was singing *Mary had a little lamb his fleece was white as snow* but Albie was trying to get his mind to go blank, to shut down the anger that was paining him in his chest. He was sure he had gone beyond anger, that it didn't matter anymore. He was sure that he was tougher than leather as he looked across the hall, over the snuffling cop's head and there, in an opposite cell, the two desperados were hanging by their necks, grinning. "You bastards," he screamed. The cop opened the door and punched him in the face. "Who the fuck you calling a bastard?" He lay on the floor for a long time. It felt good. The floor was cement. It was cold. He lay with his eyes closed. There was blood in his left eye. He didn't want to think about blood, he didn't want to think. He refused to think. He counted, 1 2 3 4 5 6 7 8 9 10 11 12 13 14...He stopped counting. Six times six is 36. It was stupid. He hummed. He crossed his ankles, he uncrossed his ankles. Though he was humming, he could see numbers. Numbers on the clock, the arrowhead hands, and St. Christopher's face between the hands, a silence. He closed that off. Like a shutter across his mind. He didn't want to think about the clock, the *tock tock tock*. He thought about Yuri's face in the clock, laughing. He wanted to laugh at the cops who thought they were so smart. The stupid cops. "Shit for brains." He'd set the timer right in front of them. He didn't want to see the time. He wanted to see a blank face. A clock that was blank. He heard a voice. He refused to look up. The bald-headed judge had refused to look up. "Since this man Starbach has no history..." In that courtroom tubular neon light, the same neon light that was in the cell, he could tell through his closed eyelids, "That man is dying." He heard a voice. "Rock-a-bye-baby, in the treetop, when the wind blows the cradle will rock..." Opening his eyes, there was a priest standing close to the other side of the bars. "Hello there," he heard the priest say. He closed his eyes. Crows. *Caw. Caw. Grief. Grief.* "He can't be real."

"Hello."

Albie refused to look. He saw a sad lonely crow in whiteface.

"Hello, hello."

It's the fucking Bell Telephone Hour, he thought.

"Just doing our Father's work..."

Holy shit, he thought. *I'm losing my mind.*

"He is your Father. And He loves you...

Albie rolled on to his side. He opened an eye. The priest was there. "You're still there," Albie said.

"Where else would I be?" the priest asked.

"Alaska," Albie said, sitting up.

"I'd like to speak to you about our Father, your Father, how He loves you."

"No, no preaching."

"No, I'm not going to preach. I'd just like you to know, in these very difficult times, that there is a love, a love as pure as a child's love."

"What else you want?"

"Nothing."

"Nobody wants nothing."

"No, no, I just want to give you these."

"So you want me to take them."

Albie sat up close to the bars, the priest was holding a basket, a Sunday collections basket, except it was filled with tiny brightly coloured books. *Gimme an E... TOMORROW IS ANOTHER DAY.*

"Take some," the priest said, and thrust the basket between the bars. Albie reached and took a handful. "What are these?" he asked.

"Parables."

"What?"

"Each little book contains one parable. They are for you to read. The parables are wonderful stories."

"You're kidding."

"No. Otherwise I wouldn't give them to you, would I?"

"How would I know?"

"These are the stories of His son who died for our sins."

"You guys never do what you say you're going to do. I said no preaching."

"I'll just leave the stories with you, and wish you well, and let you know that I'll be praying for you."

"Don't pray for me. Pray for my mother."

"Okay."

"Emma Rose. Say a prayer for Emma Rose."

"Right," and the priest, making a sign of the cross in the air, left Albie alone, clutching the little books. He opened his fist. Chicklet books. He laughed, they looked like the two-chicklet Chicklet boxes from the time when he was a kid, and he thumbed the pages. Tiny books and a big print. *The Little Parable of the Barren Fig Tree, The Little Parable of the Mustard Seed, The Little Parable of the Narrow Gate.* He closed his fist around the books and got up into a squat on his haunches. He knew a lot of time had passed. He wasn't sure how much. He had no idea how long he'd been lying on his back wild in his sorrow. He narrowed his eyes, trying to see real clear again, to part the dark waters at the back of his mind, trying to focus on a little nub of nothing until that nub amount of nothing would go away, disappear, and he would be left with only a clarity, an absolutely clear sense of the absence of everything. Concentrate. He tried so hard to concentrate that he was actually thinking of nothing, or almost nothing. But every now and then he saw his mother, Emma Rose, doomed – he was sure – to a life doing flips into the air in her chair. He blinked back tears. He could tell that he was weeping. There were tears down his cheeks. He was not sobbing. He was just weeping, overwhelmed by sorrow, thinking of the cops, how pathetic they were, the way they saw nothing and would never hear fiddle music in the trees, misunderstanding everything, and then, an enormous sense of relief took hold of him as he felt his twin, the little dwarf in his chest, cocooned in his ribcage, shrivel...shrivel and shrink into a little stone, like a peach stone, wizened the way his awful little face had always been wizened, shrunk to a stone pit, but suddenly he heard the two cops laughing and calling out, "Hey Albie, Albie, your picture's in the paper, in the *SUN*…" and they held the tabloid page open on the other side of the bars and there he was standing in the centre of the road, holding his STOP sign high with one hand and pointing with the other as the little old lady walked between cars… *"Thanks, sonny…"* and the heading over the big picture on the page opposite TODAY'S SUN-SHINE GIRL was THE CROSSING GUARD NOBODY KNOWS. *"Think nothing of it."* The cops laughed again. "Wouldn't they like to know who the real Albie is, eh?" One of the cops smacked the newspaper against the bars. "This makes me as angry as fuck," he yelled, "you'll be sorry, you little pervert shit," and Albie said very quietly, "You know what the last thing a man wants to do is?" and the cop, sniffling, his eyes swollen, said, "No," and Albie said, "The thing he does." The cops left him as he tucked his head down to his knees and began to rock on his haunches, rocking and rocking, humming the same sound over and over, waiting, thinking in the silence before the calm, *She'll know nothing, she'll know nothing, blippety – blip – blip…* rocking, rocking in the night behind his closed eyes and he could see stars, the stars in the sky are cluster bombs, a dark sky full of starlight, and then it was a little tremor that he felt first in the floor, a tremor throwing him back on his heels, followed by a rumbling that shook the building and then hearing it, even though it was 15 or 20 blocks away, a huge erupting explosion, a sound bigger than he had ever imagined, a sound that sucked the air around him and blotted out everything, the floor, the walls, the station, and it blew open the black walls of mirrors at the edge of his mind so that he saw long lines of air ducts, bent and folded to move around corners, shooting up into the air, sound tunnels, and tumbling between them, smiling and sending hand signals, his mother, Emma Rose, beaming, flying high, rising up into the air…*go in and out the window*, FOLLOW THE MADONNA… and then everything was still, though he heard yelling and phones and sirens, but everything was still, the floor was still, so he stayed on his haunches.

All his bones were shaking in his body. His body felt like a bag. An empty bag full of shaking bones. Bones dancing out of his body. He had to do something but he didn't know what to do. If he didn't do something he thought he would explode, the bag would explode, and his bones would go all over the place. The two cops would play pick-up sticks with his bones. He began to laugh, his jaw moving up and down. He opened his fist. He popped one of the little books into his mouth, biting down hard on it, chewing and chewing and this began to soothe him, the hard work of chewing soothed him, and he began to hum, *Double your pleasure double your fun, chew Wrigley's Doublemint chewing gum*, as he swallowed and then popped another little book into his mouth and started chewing. He ate three of the little books. He felt totally calm. He touched his legs, his chest, his mouth. He couldn't feel them. He couldn't feel his fingers. They were cold, ice cold. He tried to say *fingers*. He couldn't. And he couldn't think of an angry word, there was not an angry bone in his body, and he tried to spit in his hands. He wanted that sure sticky feeling. He felt a swelling in his throat, the paper, the wet words. He began to choke. He had no spit, no air, and the pressure of no air made him feel like his eyes were pushing out of his sockets and there was pain in his lungs that spread to the joints, his bones separating, and as the whole of everything began to go black in his head, he heard singing in his chest, steady and mournful, sung from far away in the hills and he heard a train whistle out by the water tower and he thought, *It's the noon train, it's come, there's no one here but me.*

Leon Rooke of Toronto is one of Canada's more prolific writers, and is the author of almost 40 books, among them *Shakespeare's Dog, The Fall of Gravity, Swinging Through Dixie, Fabulous Fictions and Peculiar Practices,* and *Oh!, Who Goes There* and *Wide World In Celebration and Sorrow* from Exile Editions. He has been widely anthologized, and has won the Governor General's Award for Fiction.